Days of Toil and Tears

The Child Labour Diary of Flora Rutherford

BY SARAH ELLIS

Scholastic Canada Ltd.

Kingston, Ontario, 1887

May 19, 1887

Dear Papa and Mama,

Make a joyful noise! I suppose in heaven you make joyful noises all the time, but make an extra one today. This morning Matron told me such good news that I hardly have the words to say how happy I am. I came right here to write to you in my notebook because if I write it down it will seem more real and fixed and not a dream. Matron had a letter from Auntie Janet. Auntie Janet had three pieces of news. The first thing is that she is married. The second thing is that she and her husband, whose name is James Duncan, have secured jobs in a big woollen mill in a town called Almonte. The third and most wonderful thing is that they have a place to live and they want me to leave Kingston and come and live with them, and work with them at the mill.

When Matron told me I managed to contain myself, but as soon as I was alone (I ran around to the vegetable garden) I cried with joy. I thought of all those joyful noises in the psalms, the sounds of harps and psalteries and timbrels. I do not exactly know what those instruments sound like, but I imagine it to be the sound inside the heart of a girl who has just found out that she will no longer live in the Protestant Orphans Home because she has a real family waiting for her. Rejoice!

Then I went inside to pare parsnips for dinner. Even parsnips for dinner cannot darken such a day.

May 20

Dear Papa and Mama,

Today I woke up early. The coal man was delivering and he is a big yelling sort of man, even before dawn. I almost turned over and went back to sleep when I remembered my news. Why waste time sleeping when I could lie awake being happy?

I took out my box of treasures. Best of the treasures are six letters from Auntie Janet, one for every birthday since I came to the Home, every one saying that she would love to have me with her, one day, when she had a home and a living. And now that one day has come.

I started to think about families. All the children here tell stories about their families, the families they remember, the families who are going to collect them some day. Most of these stories are made up. I know that because I make them up myself.

Every night, after prayers and before I go to sleep, I make up a day with you. Some things I make up from things I remember. Papa, you sing about Annie

Laurie whose throat was like a swan. Mama, you hop your fingers up my arm and recite a verse about a rabbit. You have little half-moons on your fingernails. You hold buttercups under my chin and say that I like butter. We have a dog called Laird, who runs around in circles in the snow chasing his own tail. When he trips over his feet we all laugh at the same time. One night there is a thunder and lightning storm. Laird and you, Mama, are afraid, but Papa and I are brave. We love lightning.

Some things in my made-up day are the might-have-beens. We live in a house all on our own, just our family. There is a garden. Sometimes I have brothers and sisters. I find names for them in the Bible. Jeroboam and Timothy and Zillah.

The biggest might-have-been in my story is that nobody ever gets sick and dies.

Matron sometimes says that we are a family in the Home. She especially says this when the patrons come to visit. But we all know that it isn't true.

But even with my memories and my made-up stories I do not really know what families are like. I know about moments, but not moments knitted together into days.

I thought of families in stories — stories about princesses and fairies. Princesses have families, of course — kings and queens. But mostly they seem to spend their time forbidding things or making up contests for the princess's hand in marriage. The stories don't tell about eating dinner or having rows. Fairies don't seem to have families at all. The Holy Family is a bit better because at least Joseph had a job, being a carpenter, and they went travelling and Jesus went to school and they had troubles, but no brothers and sisters and it is not quite the same, being Holy.

At church and when I go to the shops for Matron I like to look at families. Here is what I have noticed: Fathers are sometimes harsh. I hope Uncle James Duncan is not a harsh man. Sometimes brothers are very kind and sometimes they are horrid. I have never heard a mother or a father tell a child that he should be grateful to be in the family the way Matron tells us that we should be grateful to be in the Home. I wondered about families until it was time to get up.

May 21

Dear Papa and Mama,

Today I told Alice my news. It was hard. We have been friends from the very day she arrived here. It seems as though even the best news has some part in it that is sad, and leaving Alice behind is the sad part. But she was happy for me and skipped right over the sadness to a story in which she shrinks herself to the size of a fairy and goes with me in my pinafore pocket. One of the best things about Alice is that she doesn't think that eleven is too old for fairies.

May 22

Dear Papa and Mama,

In church today, in the middle of the sermon, I suddenly missed you very much. I often miss you in church because it is a place for thinking about heaven and also because I remember sitting between you in church and hearing both your voices say the prayers together. The remembering was like a flood. I started to think about going to live in a new place and I was pulled back to the time just after you died when I was sent to live at the Home. This feeling is not sensible because now I am happy as happy can be to be going to a new place, and then I was in a great despond. But sensible or not, I had to look very hard way up to the church ceiling so the tears did not spill over.

May 23

Dear Papa and Mama,

It is early. I did not sleep well last night. Harriet was coughing. When I hear coughing I think of pleurisy and that is the worst word I know. I remember when they told me you had both been "taken by pleurisy." I thought pleurisy was a kind of monster. Now that I am grown I know that it is a sickness, but in the night, in the dark, I still think of that monster when I hear coughing.

I will think of something happier, like seeing Auntie Janet.

May 24

Dear Papa and Mama,

Auntie Janet sent me some money. She wrote that James Duncan wished me to have some pocket money for my journey. I think James Duncan must be like a fairy godmother. I suppose he would be a fairy godfather, but I have never heard of such a thing. I know exactly what I will buy with the money. When next I go to the store for Matron I will get it.

Matron says that I will be leaving on Friday. How can I wait three days? Hurry up, Friday!

May 25

Dear Papa and Mama,

Time is crawling like a worm. I am thinking of worms because John C., who loves to torment me, threw a worm at me yesterday in the garden. He expected me to shriek, but I am not troubled by worms, not after having to mind so many horrid little boys. Three new ones in the Home this year and each one worse than the last. I am supposed to make them mind, but they will not. I will not miss this task for a minute. Alice tells me that she is practising her shrinking so she'll be ready to come.

May 26

Dear Papa and Mama,

Tomorrow morning I leave. Last Christmas, at the party, we had cakes sprinkled with tiny candies that Matron called hundreds and thousands. I feel like that now, a mixture of many bits. I am excited, joyful, afraid and sad too. I will miss Alice most of all, and Mary Anne and Harriet and Ellen. I will miss Cook, who is kind even when she is grumpy. I gave Alice my bead bracelet as a keepsake. Tonight the Bible reading was Psalm 148, which is a list of things praising the Lord. Sun and moon, fire and hail, creeping things and flying fowl. My favourite verse is "Praise the Lord from the earth, ye dragons, and all deeps." I think this is a good sign.

May 27

Dear Papa and Mama,

I am writing this on the train. You can see what I bought with my pocket money — this new notebook and three new pencils. The page is so clean, like new snow, and the pencils smell lovely.

The train feels much faster than it looks when you are standing watching it. It is so fast that you cannot even see near things like fences and grass. They just turn into a blur of colour and if you really try to look at them your stomach turns upside down. For a time a horse in a field galloped beside us, but we were faster. I pretended that I was on that galloping horse, racing the train. Then I pretended that I had magic boots and was running alongside the train myself, running like the wind.

Sitting across from me is a very kind and pretty lady. She has a work basket with her and when she opened it up I could not help staring. Inside were skeins and skeins of embroidery cotton in every rainbow colour, and some colours not even in the rainbow. She began to work on a fancy cloth, with purple and yellow pansies. She asked me if I did embroidery and I said no. Matron thought that good plain stitching and knitting were all we needed to learn. Then the kind lady asked me if I would like to learn. I don't know if it was proper to say yes, but I could not help myself. So she lent me a needle and some beautiful sky-blue cotton and a scrap of cloth and taught me how to do stem stitch, the lazy daisy stitch and French knots. With these three stitches I made some cunning little flowers. She lent me some scissors shaped like a long-billed bird. I like embroidery very much. It is so much more pleasant to make stitches that you want to see — unlike hemming where you are supposed to have invisible stitches. The kind lady inspected it, paying special attention to the back, and said that it was well done and that I was a quick study.

Then she said why didn't I embroider some flowers on my pinafore. At first I thought to say no, that I was not allowed to, and then I had a most bouncing thought. Matron will never know. Would Auntie Janet mind? She was not there to ask. I hesitated and the kind lady said that I must not worry, the cotton was boil-fast and the colours would not run so that no harm could come of it. She said I could use any colours I liked and that made up my mind for me.

I took off my pinafore and embroidered a line of flowers along the top of the bib. The flowers are pink, mauve and blue and the leaves are two kinds of green and the French knot middles are yellow and white. It is truly the prettiest thing I have ever worn. In between these sentences I reach up and touch it — the French knot middles are little bumps — and then I tuck my chin under and look at my own garden. I wish Alice really was in my pocket.

I long to see Auntie Janet, but I also want this train ride to go on forever. Nobody to take care of, no chores, nobody wanting anything, nobody getting into trouble, nobody to please but myself. But I must get off at Brockville and get on another train.

Later

Dear Papa and Mama,

The train from Brockville had a big surprise. We left the station and then we were plunged into utter darkness, like at the beginning of the Bible, where darkness is on the face of the deep. I could not help crying out and a voice said, "Do not distress yourself. It is just a tunnel." I was happy to come out into the light of day.

Back to my garden.

May 28, in the morning

Dear Papa and Mama,

It is Saturday morning and I can hardly believe that I am here. I woke up to the sound of a child crying. I was on my feet, thinking that it was little Jessie with her toothache, before I remembered that I wasn't at the Home. The crying sound was coming through the wall. Then I heard a woman's voice, not the words, but the sound of it. The crying has stopped now. It is early still, just a hint of daylight. No sound of Auntie or Uncle. I do not want to go back to sleep, to miss the first morning in my new home, newest morning of my whole life.

Today I am a new person. At the Home I was Flora Rutherford, orphan, or Flora Rutherford, child-minder. Now I am Flora Rutherford, niece. I did not sleep very much last night. First of all I kept waking up for the pleasure of waking up, in my own snug. (That is what Uncle James calls it, Flora's snug.) I do not ever remember sleeping in a room by myself. Nobody snuffling, nobody whimpering. And I thought it would be the quietest night of my life, but — not at all! It was the noisiest night of my life because of the trains. The first time the train whistle blew I thought it was going to come right into the house. It was that loud and close! But I don't mind. A train is a friendly noise once you know what it is. And Auntie Janet says that I will get used to it and sleep right through the noise.

But I am jumping forward. I want to tell you what happened yesterday,

As the train left Carleton Place and the conductor announced, "Next station Almonte," my heart began to fail me. I started to fret about what was coming, how my aunt and uncle are strangers to me. I thought about all the things I do not know, such as how to live in a family, how to do the work in a mill. I even started to fret about the embroidery on my pinafore. At that moment if a magic fairy had said to me, "Do you want to fly back to the Home?" I would have said yes. I am not a shy or timid girl, but I suddenly felt as though I might be.

Such fretting drained away when Auntie Janet hugged me at the train station. She hugged me and then she held me away by my shoulders for a minute and studied me, as though she were reading me, and then she said that I look just like my mother. Then her eyes got wet and shiny. Then a handsome young man with black curly hair appeared and it was Uncle James. He took off his cap and bowed very low and said, "Welcome, Lady Flora," and I didn't know if he was mocking me. But Auntie Janet laughed and said, "Oh, go on with you, you daft silly," and she told me that he was always like this and that I wasn't to mind him.

It was a very short walk from the station to the place where Auntie Janet and Uncle James live. I suppose I must say where *I* live now. The building is three stories tall and our rooms are on the second floor. There are two rooms. One is a kitchen and sitting room, and a little curtained-off corner for me. The other is a bedroom. The bathroom is downstairs and we share it with the other people who live in the building. In the sitting room there is a stove, a woodbox, a sink with a shelf above, and a dresser for crockery. There is a table and three chairs. In my corner there is a bed and a hook for my clothes and a box under the bed for my things. There are pretty things to look at — two fancy teacups, a tatted cover for the table, a picture of flowers on the wall and a rag rug. I told Auntie Janet about the embroidery lady on the train and she admired my pinafore and said that she will teach me how to tat and make rag rugs if I like.

Auntie Janet made tea and then she and Uncle James told me a bit about the mill, the Almonte Woollen Mill. Auntie is a spinner and Uncle is a weaver. I am to be a doffer girl, which is something in the spinning room with Auntie, but I couldn't quite understand what. They told me that it is the largest woollen mill in Canada and that the worsted cloth they make has won prizes for quality. Auntie Janet said that the Prime Minister might be wearing a suit that she helped to make. "Yes," said Uncle James, "if it were not for Janet and me, Sir John A. Macdonald might be going around wrapped in a sheepskin!"

I asked if we would go to work tomorrow, but Uncle James said the mill owner, Mr. Flanagan, had declared a holiday because Lady Flora had come to Almonte. Then Auntie Janet pretended to punch him in the arm and said that the mill was closed for one day while they replaced some machinery, but that it was lucky timing because it gave them a chance to welcome me.

Last thing. I was writing in my snug corner when Auntie Janet put her head round the curtain. She asked me what I was writing. I've never told anyone about these letters to you because I feared I would be mocked, so I thought to say that I was writing a journal. But I did not want to lie to her, when she is so kind to take me in, so I just told her. She smiled and said wasn't I clever to be able to write such long letters. She said that she found writing hard and that made me even more grateful for the letters she sent me.

Uncle James piped up and said, "You wrote plenty of letters when we found out that Flora was coming." Auntie Janet looked shy and said, "Well, I wanted to share the good news with all the family." Then she kissed me goodnight, which was surprising and nice. I wonder if she will do that every night? I am not accustomed to kissing. There was not much kissing at the Home. Only the bread man with the lumpy red nose and greasy hair who tried to kiss me when he brought the bread in the morning. I didn't like that one bit.

So the first thing I have discovered about families is that there is teasing, but not mocking.

One more last thing. The nicest thing about Auntie Janet is the way she smells. That sounds disrespectful, but I mean that she smells lovely.

There's another train coming through, rattling the walls. What will today be like?

Still May 28, in the evening

Dear Papa and Mama,

If there were a pleasanter day to be had I cannot think what it would be. Auntie made porridge for breakfast and it had no lumps, which is something that Cook at the Home could not manage. I was helpful with stirring and washing up and fetching water. I am determined to be very helpful. I started to sweep, but then Uncle said it was a holiday and we should leave off sweeping and go out and introduce me to the town.

The first thing I got introduced to and got introduced to me was a neighbour. As we came out the front door there was a boy shooting marbles against the wall. He jumped up and said, "At last! Are you Flora?" Uncle James laughed and said that the boy was Murdo Campbell and that the Campbells are our neighbours.

"We live through the wall," said Murdo. "There are seven of us." Then he rattled off seven names which I do not remember except that he is the second oldest. Auntie Janet said that the Campbells are like a flights of stairs. The remarkable thing about Murdo is that he has the brightest red hair I've ever seen. In the sun it looked as though his head were on fire — half boy, half candle. Murdo said that he had been waiting for me to arrive. "All the rest of them are too small to be any use," he said, "except Kathleen, and she's too bossy. Isn't it grand to have a day's holiday?"

I was not sure what I was to be of use for, but Auntie and Uncle seemed to be friendly with Murdo and he tagged right along with us, talking a mile a minute, cheerful as can be.

We walked along past the railway station and then onto Bridge Street and Mill Street to the river. Auntie and Uncle pointed out all the buildings: boot maker, blacksmith, grocery store, dry goods store, hotel, tinsmith, drugstore, town hall, dentist, surgeon, post office and watchmaker. Next to the hotel was a long line of stables and carriage sheds. I like the sounds of horses — the jingling of harness and that sneezing sound they make with their noses. Murdo told stories about who lives where and which shopkeepers are kind and which are mean.

When we got to the town hall, which is very grand, Murdo pointed out the electric light and Uncle James laughed and said all the courting couples meet there. "It's a spooning light," he said and Auntie Janet laughed and Murdo groaned.

Then we got to the river. It is splendid. It is called the Mississippi (when you are writing that word it is hard to know when to stop) and it has a tremendous waterfall. The water comes down the river looking lazy and smooth and then when it gets to the falls it turns white and boiling and racing. I thought of horses with great white manes.

Murdo tried to explain how the power of the river turns the wheel, which is the power for all the machines in the woollen mill. He was very enthusiastic and he started talking about overshot wheels and undershot wheels and I didn't understand it at all, but Auntie told me I would see it on Monday, which was time enough to be thinking about the mill.

On the way home we bought some groceries and then Murdo disappeared to play baseball and Uncle James went off to go fishing.

Auntie and I went home and had a cup of tea. She showed me her knitting project, a sweater for Uncle James. I told her that I knew how to knit socks, even to turning the heels, because Matron was very stern about girls learning to knit. Auntie was very impressed. She found some grey wool, suitable for socks, and some needles for me, and suggested we take our work outside.

We walked to the other side of the river and found a place to sit in the sun, looking across at the mill. It looks like a huge castle, with the sun shining on the windows and the river like a moat. I thought of a princess living in the castle. She would have a whole room full of gowns, in all the colours of the autumn leaves. Crimson, golden, fiery orange, yellowy-green and bright pink. She would have a different crown for every day of the week.

As we knitted, Auntie told me a story. It was about a bairn (that's a baby), who was stolen away by the fairies. The mother was beside herself with grief. But a wise woman told her to make a cloak that was so beautiful that she could trade it for her baby. Luckily the woman was a weaver. She wove a cloak from goose down. It was so soft and white it could have been a cloud caught from the sky. Then, using her own golden hair, she wove in a border of flowers and fruits and magical beasts. The fairies were so taken with this cloak that they were lured into returning the baby. It all ended happily.

Auntie is a wonderful storyteller. She makes magic as everyday as parsnips. After a few minutes I was in two places at once — Almonte and the land where fairies are. I asked her how she could remember stories so well and she told me that she learned the stories from her grandmother. "You remember the things you heard when you were small," she said. She told me about her grandmother, who is my great-grandmother, and how she came from Scotland to Canada on a great ship. "They could not bring much with them, but the stories were light." She said that she liked that story because the heroine was a weaver, just like Uncle James.

I liked the cloak in the story. I could see it in my mind. I also liked what the wise woman said to the mother: "My wisdom is only as old as man, but the wisdom of the fairies is older than the beginning of the world." Alice would like this story too. I wonder what she is doing at this minute.

When we got home we met another family that lives in our building. They are just two. Granny Whitall lives with her grandson, who is a grown-up man. She takes care of small children, like the small Campbells, when their parents work at the mill. Auntie Janet said that even though Granny Whitall is very old she is still wonderful at sewing, just needing help with threading the needles.

Fish for dinner.

There is one more thing about the day, but my hand is just too tired to write.

May 29, in the morning

Dear Papa and Mama,

Again I'm awake before Auntie and Uncle. So I will tell you the one last thing from yesterday.

In the evening Auntie Janet went into a trunk and brought out a Bible. Inside the front cover are written the names of the family, from now and long ago. The first name I noticed was my own. *Flora Rutherford, b. 1875.* Alongside were the names of my three brothers, who died as infants. Above it were your names, *William Rutherford, b. 1851 d. Oct. 1881,* and *Sarah Dow, b. 1855, m. William Rutherford 1873, d. Oct. 1881.* A sadness came upon me on reading those names. I think of you every day, but I think of you as angels. Seeing your names in the Bible made me think of you alive and walking on the earth with all the other people.

Auntie Janet pointed out the name of Martha Dow, her grandmother: *b. 1802 Glasgow, Scotland, d. 1873, Pakenham Township, Ontario, Canada.* "There she is, the one who told the stories."

Auntie Janet told me that Granny Dow knew more stories than there are days in a year. "They just came out of her mouth like water over a millrace," she said. "She was a tiny wee woman, but when she told stories she could quiet a whole room of great big men. I think she had the stories from the fairies themselves. She always said it was a pity that the fairies were disappearing because of us building great cities and driving them away."

I ran my fingers over the lovely loopy writing and thought about all those people in the olden days.

When Uncle James came home he said that it was fleece-scouring night. "We'll dip you in the carbolic," he said, "and get you ready for the carding room." But Auntie Janet said that he wasn't to terrify me with such talk and that all he meant was that it was bath night. Which is one thing that is the same as at the Home.

There's that baby crying again, through the wall. It must be a Campbell. Probably teething. Sun's up so I'm going to get up and be helpful. I watched Uncle James yesterday and now I think I know how to light the stove.

May 29, in the evening

Dear Papa and Mama,

So much is new that if I were to write about it all I would not have time to be living it through, but only writing about it! I made the tea this morning and had it ready when Auntie got up. She said she felt like Queen Victoria.

I know you will want to know about church. Auntie and Uncle go to St. John's Church. It was grand, walking into church just with Auntie and Uncle, and not in a line the way we did from the Home, with everyone staring at us.

Last night I thanked God for Auntie and Uncle and this morning I thanked Him again and asked Him to give me a grateful heart.

Most things about church, like the words and the hymns and the books, were the same. Just like in Kingston there were girls my age with nice dresses and just like in Kingston they did not look friendly.

The most surprising and different thing was the sermon. The minister was not the regular minister, but a visitor. He preached on the text "the labourer is worthy of his hire." But he did not just talk about Bible times. He talked about now and he said something about how his blood boiled when he saw wealthy men "grinding their employees in the dirt." He had a great black beard and his beard started to move up and down more and more when he said things like, "beastly, diabolical doctrine." He is very different from Rev. Pollock at home, who always spoke very softly and only about Bible times.

On the walk home Auntie said that she thought the minister was too fierce and she hoped he wasn't talking about Mr. Flanagan, who owns the mill, because Mr. Flanagan is a decent man and doesn't grind the mill workers in the dirt, but pays good wages. But Uncle said that the minister had spoken a lot of good sense, and besides, he liked a sermon that didn't put him to sleep. Then Uncle asked if Auntie liked the minister's whiskers and perhaps he should grow a fine beard like that, and Auntie said that she would not like it one bit because she would not care to kiss a man with whiskers. I agree.

In the afternoon Auntie put together a big pot of beans to last us all week. She says that there isn't much time for cooking in the week so she cooks a big pot of something on Sunday afternoon.

After supper Auntie said she wanted to ask me a favour. She seemed shy to ask and I could not imagine what it could be. Running an errand? Sewing? Scrubbing? As it turned out, she wanted me to read aloud to her and Uncle James. "Mr. Campbell usually shares his newspaper with us," she said, "but James doesn't read, and I'm not good at reading aloud. We thought you might be." She pulled out *The Almonte Gazette.*

I wanted to do it, but I faced a dilemma. Was it right to read a newspaper on Sundays? Matron would not let us read anything but Bible stories on Sundays, and a book about being good called *The Peep of Day.* I did not know what to say.

Auntie Janet saw right away that something was wrong and she just asked me straight out so I told her. Then we three all talked about it and decided that I would read aloud from the Bible first and then I would read the newspaper. When we talked about it Uncle James and Auntie Janet really listened to what I had to say. Is this what happens in families?

I asked what I should read from the Bible and Uncle James said, right away, that it should be Judges, Chapter 6. This was a story about a man called Gideon and it had sheep fleeces in it. A bit hard to read with words like Abi-ezrite, but I did my best. Auntie Janet teased Uncle James that he only attends to the Bible reading when there is something about sheep and wool. Uncle James said that that wasn't true. He said that he always attends with one ear. It is just that when there is something about wool or weaving or fishing or something else that he knows about, he attends with both ears. I know just what he means. I attend with one ear almost all the time (except when I'm daydreaming, such as when the lesson is about begats or smiting), but when there is mention of an angel I get both ears working. Angels and fairies are my favourite things in stories. (And princesses.)

Then I read some parts of the newspaper. A boy was attacked by a dog. There was a fire in Irishtown. Maple syrup costs a dollar a gallon.

Uncle James says that I am such a good reader that I could be a minister myself if I would only grow a beard. I know he is being comical, but it still made me feel very happy. I don't recall that anybody has ever told me I am good at something.

Right before bed Auntie said she had to talk to me about something very important. She looked so stern that I wondered if I had done something wrong. But she was not angry, just serious. She told me that when I am working at the mill I must always be careful. She told me that the machinery is dangerous. "All mill accidents are bad accidents," she said, "and it only takes a moment's inattention. Promise me that you will always pay attention, watch where you are going, and never never run." I promised.

And now to sleep. Tomorrow will be my first day as a doffer girl. I asked Auntie and Uncle to be sure to wake me up early early, but they smiled and said I needn't worry about that and I would find out why in the morning.

May 30

Dear Papa and Mama,

Now I understand why I did not need to be routed out in the morning. I was fast asleep when the noise of bells got into my dream. (It was a very curious dream about my teeth falling out. When they fell on the ground they made a little ringing noise. This was not frightening, just odd.) But then my teeth jumped right back into my head in a great hurry when I awoke to the sound of bells filling the air. When Auntie Janet put her head round the curtain she was laughing. "Welcome to Almonte," she said, "town of mill bells."

Auntie Janet told Uncle James that he had to make the porridge because she had another important job. And he pretended to be cross. She took no notice. Then she braided my hair. She said I needed to have it pulled back to work at the mill because otherwise it is dangerous — loose hair could get caught in the machinery. She was very gentle with the brushing and the braiding. I almost fell back to sleep. My hair has always been a trial, for it is thick and the kind of curly that tangles easily. One of the first things I remember from the Home is a nurse brushing my hair so roughly that I thought she was going to scalp me. She called it "wicked gypsy hair." But Auntie Janet said it was lovely and Uncle James said it was like a number-one quality fleece and I had better watch out when I walked through the wool sorting room.

Auntie Janet made two braids and then she made rings of them. I've never had this before, tidy and pretty both. With her own hair she did this twisting thing and it all ended up in a neat roll on the top of her head.

We had porridge (Uncle James can also make it without lumps) and Auntie packed bread and cheese into three pails and then we set off. First we walked along the road by the railway tracks, tracks on one side and rail sheds on the other. There were birds singing and flowers in the grass. As soon as we got onto Mill Street there was a river of people, all going to work. Some people were walking and talking cheerfully and some looked as though they were still asleep or wished to be. This is just like the Home. There are people who like to get up early and people who like to stay up late. Matron was like a bird in the morning, poking her beak into everything. Cook was like a slow turtle. And grumpy first thing.

On Mill Street I heard running steps and Murdo came up alongside. He told me that I looked like a proper mill girl with my lunch pail and all. We stopped for a minute on the bridge. The waterfall, roaring and bubbling white over the rocks, was sending jewels of water into the air. But then the mill bell began to ring again and Uncle James said we had to hurry. We walked by two mills and some of the river of people went in those gates and then a red-painted building that Auntie told me was a knitting mill, where they make long underwear. "They call it Big Red," said Murdo. Finally we went down a little hill to the Almonte Woollen Mill No. 1, which is OUR mill.

It looked even taller close up — bigger than a train station, bigger than a church. There was a crowd of people mingling outside, men and women, some boys and girls too. Auntie Janet greeted many of them and they said, "So this is Flora."

This all takes longer to write about than to walk as it is only about fifteen minutes distance. Auntie says it seems long enough on a bitter dark winter morning. But it is so hard to imagine winter in summer. As hard to imagine sad when you're happy. And the other way round is true too. Why is that? Now I haven't

May 31

Dear Papa and Mama,

The letter from yesterday ended in the middle of a sentence because I fell asleep. Auntie Janet said I just fell forward onto my notebook. She had to get me out of my clothes and put me to bed just as though I were a baby. I do remember being tired. I was tired in my arms and tired in my mind. The clattering noise of the machines made it hard to fix my mind on learning new things. I am determined to do everything well and not disappoint Auntie Janet. Tonight I am not so tired, so I will finish my story about Flora's first day:

At seven o'clock a loud bell rang and we all went in. Uncle James headed off up the stairs and Murdo and some other boys ran across the yard toward a shed. Auntie and I stopped at an office. There was a man wearing a suit sitting at a desk. The man asked me my name and he wrote it in a big book. Then he said that he knew I would be a good worker because Auntie and Uncle were excellent operatives. Then he said that Auntie was to take me to see Mr. Haskin. Then Auntie said thank you and I said thank you. As we started up the stairs I asked Auntie if the man was Mr. Flanagan who owns the mill, and she laughed. "No," she said, "the likes of us don't see too much of Mr. Flanagan, especially at seven o'clock in the morning. That was Mr. Boothroyd."

We went up and up the stairs. We stopped at the fourth floor to look into the weaving room where Uncle works. I didn't know it would be so noisy. The big machines make a great bang and clatter. There were many men and women working and I saw Uncle, but he didn't look up to see us.

Then we went up one more flight and came to the spinning room. The room is very large with tall windows all along one side. Long belts loop down from the high ceiling and are attached to machinery. It was noisy in that room too, but more of a loud hum that just goes on and on. Not so much of a clatter. It seemed to be all women in that room and they looked up at me as I came in. Some smiled.

The room was very warm, which felt good early in the morning, but not by noon. I wondered why we could not open the windows, but Auntie said it needs to be warm and damp so the threads do not break. The air was filled with bits of wool, like a snowstorm. The women have wool clinging to their clothes and their hair. If you stayed there long enough you would start to look like a sheep.

Another man in a suit came up to us. Mr. Haskin. Everything about him was thin, even his nose and lips. He and Auntie talked, but I couldn't hear a word they were saying. So I just nodded and tried to look like an excellent operative.

Auntie took me over to the spinning machine. It is a wonder. There is a frame that stays in one place and a carriage that moves back and forth on rails. It all looks a bit like a dance. The machine pulls out the threads, many at a time, and makes them thinner and at the same time it twists them to make them strong. In the olden days women would spin at spinning wheels and they could only make one thread at a time.

Auntie spoke right into my ear so that I could hear her and she told me my job. I am to take the full bobbins off the spindles and replace them with empty ones. This is called doffing. When I was carrying the bobbins in their wooden box to the right place I saw another girl, smaller than me, doing the same job. I smiled but she just looked at the floor in a timid way.

At ten o'clock there was a loud bell. This is when we have a break for a rest and to use the toilet. When they turned off the machines the silence was louder than the sound. I felt as though I had silence clouds around my ears stuffing them up.

I met the other spinning frame operatives. Mrs. Brown is a stern-looking woman with a turned-down mouth. She is a widow and her two sons and one daughter work at the mill. Then there are Mrs. Murphy and Miss Bertha Rose. A smiling woman with dark red hair I guessed to be Mrs. Campbell, even before she told me. "I've already heard a lot about you from Murdo," she said. "You will have discovered that Murdo talks like this machine spins — he never tires!"

The other doffer girl is called Ann. She does not have much to say.

The friendliest and prettiest operative is a young woman, younger than Auntie Janet, named Agnes Bamford. Ann and I are the only girls. The break went very quickly and at the end Mr. Haskin came in. He gave a little speech in a thin voice about working hard. When he turned his back to leave I saw Agnes make a funny face. She saw me seeing her and winked at me.

Another loud bell at noon told us that it was time for dinner. We took our dinner outside to eat. There is a garden next to the mill for the mill workers, and a cricket pitch for the men. It was quiet and it felt good to breathe outside air. Murdo and some other boys who work in the dye house played catch. Three girls from the weave room talked among themselves. I tried to talk to Ann, saying that the wool made me think of snow, but she just said, "No, that's not right. Snow is cold." There's not much you can reply to that.

Agnes came to sit with Auntie and me and she asked all sorts of questions. Where was I from? Where had I been? What had I seen? "I'm just longing to go anywhere," she said, "anywhere but Carp and Almonte." I noticed that Auntie Janet wasn't too friendly to Agnes. Polite enough, but distant. The half hour passed by in a second and my ears were barely unplugged before we went back into the racket.

Then it was the same until six o'clock when another bell rang and that was a very welcome sound. One the walk home Auntie told me that every time she caught sight of me in the day her heart danced. "Almost everyone has family here," she said, "and it is just grand to have one of my own people here with me." I could not seem to say this, but I am happy just to be somebody's people.

Today was much the same except that I met Murdo's father and all six brothers and sisters, Kathleen, Percy, Archie, Willie, John and baby Bea. Kathleen works in the weave room. They all have some kind of red hair. Mr. Campbell works in the dye house. Uncle James says he must take his children there when they are babies and dip their heads in cochineal. (Cochineal is red.)

One more thing. I forgot to tell you about someone else at the mill. It is Smokey the spinning-room cat. Her job is to catch mice so that they don't eat our dinners! She is soft and grey and her tongue is very raspy. Agnes said that Mr. Flanagan could fire all the carders and just let Smokey lick the wool into shape.

June 1

Dear Papa and Mama,

The day is done and darkness falls from the wings of night. Isn't this a fine way of saying that it is nighttime? It is poetry. It is from a poem by Mr. Henry Wadsworth Longfellow.

In the spinning room some of the operatives have pieces cut out of newspapers, or hand-written, stuck on to their machines. Auntie told me that they were poems or songs or hymns that the operatives were learning by heart. We are not allowed to bring books to the mill to read, but Mr. Haskin does not mind the paste-ups. The day is full of short periods of time, just long enough to read a line or two, when you are not really doing anything, but you cannot leave the machine.

This day is done poem is pasted up on Agnes's machine so every time I doff it I try to learn one more line. Here is the first verse:

The day is done, and the darkness
Falls from the wings of Night.
As a feather is wafted downward
From an eagle in his flight.

Longfellow is a good name. I wonder if he was tall? What would it be like if our names described one thing about the way we look? The visiting minister at St. John's would be Rev. Bigbeard. Murdo would be Mr. Flamehead and I would be Miss Flora Sheepfleecehair. Mr. Haskin would be Mr. Pinch-nose.

I have a lot of practice with naming because of naming fairies. Of course eleven is far too old for fairies, especially as I am a mill operative, but nobody knows except you (and Alice.) My main fairies are Moon-Shadow and Sundew, who are beautiful and good, and Bladderwort, who is bad. I wonder if Alice will keep on with her fairies. Harriet and Ellen didn't have much time for make believe.

I do miss Alice. I try to be friendly with Ann, but she seems a very dull girl. Her father works in the repair shop. He is very silent, with stern eyebrows and he does not seem to pay Ann much mind.

June 2

Dear Papa and Mama,

Last night I had a bad dream of the mill. All the bobbins were filling up faster and faster and then falling off the machine and everything was getting tangled. I tried and tried to replace them, but my legs felt as if they were pushing through deep snow and then all the wool in the air really turned into deep snow and my feet were freezing. Then I woke up and I was so so glad to be back in the world and not in my dream. I told Auntie Janet about the dream and she said that she gets that dream, that every spinner gets that dream, of not being able to keep up. On the way to work she told me and Uncle James a comical story about a man who gets a magic porridge pot and it just keeps bubbling out porridge because he has forgotten the magic words to make it stop, until the porridge is running down the streets. Uncle James started to say all the words he knew for stop, like halt and cease and "Quit, you blessed porridge!" Uncle James is cheery so early in the morning.

Later, when the working day was over and we were all pouring out of the mill and up the road, I felt as though we were a river of magic porridge.

The verse for today was:

I see the lights of the village
Gleam through the rain and the mist,
And a feeling of sadness comes o'er me
That my soul cannot resist.

I think that Long Fellow is a good poet. Sometimes a feeling of sadness comes o'er me too, but not today, which turned out to be a happy one.

It was also a useful day, as I learned how to rescue a turtle. On the way home we saw a large snapping turtle on the road near the river. They are the most odd and ancient-looking creatures, with claws like bears. Uncle said it was likely looking for a nesting site and that it didn't stand a chance of crossing the road with all the horses and wagons. So he picked it up and carried it. "Use two hands," he said, "and pick it up from the back, with the tail between your hands. And don't get in range of those jaws." I will remember that if I ever decide to help a snapping turtle cross the road, but I probably won't.

June 3

Dear Papa and Mama,

I think Auntie Janet is the kindest person in the world. Not kind in the way that the Home visitors were kind, but kind and jolly, which is different. This evening we were washing some clothes and she noticed my flour-sack drawers. At the Home we made all our underwear out of feed sacks. Feed sacks are made of good strong stuff and sometimes they are even pretty colours, but sometimes they have words on them and no matter how many times you wash them or how long you leave them in the sun to bleach, the words still show. I ended up with a pair of drawers that said something embarrassing on them.

When Auntie Janet saw them she did not laugh. She just said that *So-Big Flour* was an unfortunate thing to have printed on your underwear, but luckily nobody sees it. So then I just had to tell her the story about the time I slipped on the ice while going to the store and before I could get my dress pulled down that horrid boy who helps the coal man saw the *So-Big Flour* words and he mocked me and how I wanted to sink into the earth and disappear. Auntie Janet said that there is nothing more horrid than horrid boys. Then we went on washing for a bit. Then she said, "Of course it could have been worse. It could have said *Best Hog Feed.*" Then we laughed until we were crying. Auntie Janet said we must stop before we got the washing water salty, but we couldn't.

After the washing I read out loud from the newspaper. I read serious and dull things and then I read that Mr. Gomersill has put in a Bell telephone and that there are twenty-one subscribers to the telephone exchange in Arnprior. Then I read about a man who married two wives. When the wives found out, they got together and attacked the man with an axe and a broomstick. Uncle James asked Auntie Janet what she would do if she found out that he had another wife and she said she would push him out in the Mississippi in a canoe with no paddle. He said that didn't sound so bad and then she said that she would do it just above the falls.

June 4

Dear Papa and Mama,

Today was payday and half day. We finish at noon and then we go to the paymaster's desk. Of course I do not get wages yet because I am still learning, but Auntie Janet said that I had been a great help to her and so she gave me twenty cents and said I could buy whatever I liked. I knew right away what I wanted so I went to the dry goods store. I bought a paper of embroidery needles and then, after much much thinking and choosing, three skeins of embroidery cotton. I picked apple green, rose and forget-me-not blue.

On the way home I was frightened by a one-armed man sitting outside the livery stable with a skinny yellow dog. When I passed by he yelled out, sharp and angry. I just about dropped the shopping. Later Uncle told me that the man's name is Barney. He lost his arm in an accident at the mill years ago, and after the accident the young woman he was engaged to wouldn't have him and then he just got more and more bitter and now he doesn't talk. He just yells. The liveryman gives him a bed and food. Uncle said he's harmless, but I'm going to walk on the other side of the street just the same.

June 5

Dear Papa and Mama,

A feeling of sadness has come o'er me. I got up early this morning and I decided to have a drink of water from one of the pretty teacups. But as I was taking it down from the shelf I knocked it and the saucer cracked. It is not in pieces, but if you look carefully you can see the crack. Auntie only has two of these cups. They have orange sunflowers on them and a bit of gold on the edge. Now one is spoiled. I did not want to own up to my carelessness so I just put the cup and saucer back on the shelf. When Auntie uses them next will she notice? Will she know that I did it? I am careless and deceitful. I cannot write any more about this.

June 5 (later)

Dear Papa and Mama,

All through church I could not think of anything but the saucer. Every prayer and every reading seemed to be directed right at me. I could not even enjoy the hymns. The ordinary minister was back. His name is Rev. Parfitt. He is young and clean-shaven. The sermon was not as interesting as last week and I could not listen at all. All I could think about was that Auntie and Uncle would be angry and send me back to the Home. When we came out from church it was raining and that seemed a punishment for me as well.

After lunch Uncle James went off somewhere and I just dreaded that Auntie Janet would suggest we have tea from the fancy cups. At the same time I hoped she would suggest it so that we could get it over with. When she finally said did I want a cup of tea I just burst into tears. At the Home I became very good at never crying, but all the kindness here in Almonte has made me weak.

Of course then I told her everything. She looked at the saucer and said that I mustn't be distressed and that she would show me the magic trick of mending cracked china. She put the saucer in a saucepan of milk and put it on the fire. "We'll simmer that for a few hours," she said, "and all will be well." And it was. You could not even tell it had been cracked. My heart is mended too.

June 6

Dear Papa and Mama,

I've got one more verse by heart from Mr. Longfellow:

A feeling of sadness and longing,
That is not akin to pain,
And resembles sorrow only
As the mist resembles the rain.

I think this is about big sad and little sad. But I am neither today because I have done well at work. Mr. Haskin gave me an extra job. Sometimes when the carriage moves away from the frame one of the threads breaks. My job is to follow the carriage as it moves back toward the frame, pick up the two ends and twist them together again. This is called piecing. The good thing about this job is that you don't know when you will have to do it, so it is not as tedious as doffing. The bad thing about it is that you don't know when you will have to do it, so you have to pay more attention. But I am glad for the extra job. Auntie says I should be proud of myself because I have shown that I am a good worker after only one week.

Ann is even more silent than usual. I think she is put out because of my new job. I don't know what to do about that.

Your daughter, Flora Rutherford, doffer and piecer

June 7

Dear Papa and Mama,

Smokey has disappeared. All morning I expected to feel her winding around my legs. At the break I asked the weave room ladies if they had seen her, but they hadn't. She did not appear all day. I have only known Smokey a week, but already I miss her. I have always wanted a cat. Once Ellen McAnally at the Home found a stray kitten, but Matron would not let us keep it. We promised that we would take care of it and give it part of our own food, but she said it would be too much bother. I know it is wrong to hate, but I did hate Matron then.

The other news is from Agnes. She had it from her cousin, who is a spinner at the mill in Sherbrooke. We are to have commissioners at the mill, commissioners from the government. They will ask us questions and then they will write it all up in a big report that the Prime Minister will read.

We wondered what they will ask, and she said they will ask us about our wages and our hours and such.

Agnes says they will talk to everyone and they will write it all down. Mrs. Brown snorted and said, "Talk to the likes of us? That'll happen the next day after never." I think Mrs. Brown must be right. They will speak to Mr. Flanagan surely, or perhaps Mr. Haskin, but I don't think the Prime Minister will want to read about me. I think Mr. Flanagan will have them to tea in the office and we will not see them at all.

Uncle James says that he wishes the commissioners would stop and inspect Bessie Murphy. When I asked why he just rolled his eyes. So, at dinnertime, I asked the weave room trio and they told me the whole story. Bessie Murphy is the room girl in Uncle James's weave room and she is very mean to Lizzie Bruce. Seems that Lizzie Bruce is the cousin to Mary Bruce and Mary Bruce stole away Bessie Murphy's beau. So, when Lizzie's loom has a problem Bessie won't go untangle the warp for ages and ages and that puts Lizzie behind in her work and makes for bad feeling all through the room. But I don't think the Prime Minister will want to know about this.

June 8

Dear Papa and Mama,

I am learning a great deal by reading *The Almonte Gazette* to Uncle James and Auntie Janet. It comes out on Fridays and lasts us all week. Tonight I read about the plans to celebrate Queen Victoria's Jubilee. This year she has been the queen for fifty years. She rules over the British Empire, which has 250 million people. In the paper it said that she sets an example to us all, "frowning down anything antagonistic to pure life." This took us quite a while to understand, even after I sounded out "antagonistic." I think I finally figured out that she must be something like Mrs. Brown, who frowns down men like Frank Coleman who say rude things to the female operatives. Except that Queen Victoria does this all over the world. Uncle James says that that is a lot of frowning. The newspaper also said we are lucky to be living in such a favoured and progressive age.

The Almonte celebration will be on June 21. Great things are planned, such as a parade and sports and concerts. Then came the best news. Right there in the paper it said that Mr. Flanagan will close Almonte Woollen Mill No. 1 for the whole day so that everyone can attend the celebration.

I've learned another verse of Mr. Longfellow's poem:

Come, read to me some poem,
Some simple and heartfelt lay,
That shall soothe this restless feeling,
And banish the thoughts of day.

June 9

Dear Papa and Mama,

It is easy to daydream at work. The noise makes you stay inside your own mind. Sometimes I daydream about riding a horse beside a rushing train. Sometimes I daydream about living in a grand house, wearing a beautiful silk gown and spending my day arranging flowers and reading poetry. Sometimes I daydream about being a fairy, who goes around making things better for everybody by magic. I fly with Sundew when she turns sunlight into gold for all the beggars and with Moon-Shadow when she touches down on sick people in the night and makes them well.

All these daydreams have a family in them, a horse-riding family, a rich family, a fairy family.

June 10

Dear Papa and Mama,

Agnes has more to say about the commissioners She says she is going to tell them all our complaints. Then when the Prime Minister reads the report he will make sure that justice is done. She says that she is going to tell the commissioners about getting locked out when we are late and about the time when some man threw a bobbin over the partition between the men's and women's water closets and how she is sure it was Frank Coleman and how the partition isn't high enough anyway.

That was too much for Mrs. Braidwood, the weaver. "You're not going to talk to those commissioners about the toilet!" she said. But Agnes put on her face like stone and said she was because there should properly be a toilet just for the women at the far end of the room so that we didn't have to put up with the beastly behaviour of men.

I learned another verse of the poem today:

Not from the grand old masters,
Not from the bards sublime,
Whose distant footsteps echo
Through the corridors of Time.

June 11

Dear Papa and Mama,

Payday and I earned $1.60! We lined up at the paymaster's desk and he gave us our wages. I signed my name in his book, which is on a high desk. The paymaster is a very cheerful man. I suppose if you give people money every week that makes them happy and then that happiness bounces back to you. When it came to my turn he asked me if I knew how to write. I said I did and then I made sure to sign my name most carefully.

Walking home with my coins in my pinafore pocket, I saw some schoolgirls skipping. I like to skip and for just a moment I wanted to be with them, playing. They had very pretty dresses. But then I looked down at the flowers on my pinafore and I jingled the coins in my pocket. They are just children, but I am a mill girl even if I do have to stand on the bobbin box to reach the desk to sign my name.

I wish that you could see what a person I have become. Perhaps you do look down and see.

Uncle James and I gave our wages to Auntie Janet, who takes care of paying the rent and buying what we need.

June 12

Dear Papa and Mama,

Today in church I suddenly missed Alice so much. I missed her sitting beside me. I missed sewing with her on Sunday afternoons. I missed talking about Sundew and Bladderwort. Auntie Janet is kind as can be. Murdo is comical. Agnes is fun. The weave room trio are nice enough, especially when we talk about the disappearance of Smokey. But they are not the same as one true friend.

June 13

Dear Papa and Mama,

Today was a vexing day. I suspect that Bladderwort is behind it all. I burnt the porridge and had to wash the pot and start over and a button came off my dress just as I was getting ready and I had to sew that back on and that made me later and later. Uncle James was impatient and left without us. Then, just as Auntie and I were at the top of Mill Street, I suddenly had to use the toilet, in a hurry. Home was closer than the mill so I said that Auntie should go on ahead and I would catch up. I ran as fast as I could, both directions, but when I got to the mill the bell was quiet and the door was locked. I looked up at the clock over the door. It was three minutes past seven. I remembered the rule. If you are late then the door is locked until ten minutes after seven and you lose pay. I felt very ashamed standing about waiting to be let in and having my name recorded. When I made it up to the spinning room Agnes winked at me, which was kind, but it was as if hobgoblins had invaded. One of the machines jammed, there seemed to be broken threads every minute, I could not keep up with the doffing and in our morning hurry both Auntie and I had forgotten our dinner pails. At noon I ran home to fetch them, but then we only had a few minutes to gobble down our dinner and all afternoon I felt as though I had rocks in my stomach.

Being in trouble this morning made me feel I was back in the Home. There, I was often in trouble because the little ones got into something. I hate being in trouble, but here at least I'm not blamed for somebody else. And at the end of the day, even though I am so tired, there is just Auntie and Uncle and me, and a different place to go.

Where is Smokey?

June 14

Dear Papa and Mama,

Smokey has reappeared. With kittens! She had made a little home for them in the wool bin. Between jobs I went to visit them. There are four of them. They are so tiny and dear. Their eyes are closed and their ears stick tight to their heads. Two tabbies, one plain grey and one with a bit of every colour that cats come in. The many-coloured one licked my fingers. Tomorrow I am going to bring a bit of cream for Smokey.

June 15

Dear Papa and Mama,

I am the happiest girl in Lanark County. I have a kitten of my own. Halleluia!

When today started there was no way to know that it would end so happily. Here is what happened.

Late this afternoon Smokey got herself caught up in the spinning machinery. I saw her first. I could see that she was tangled in the wool and that she was about to be hurt. I screamed out, but at first nobody heard me because it is so noisy. Then Agnes saw me jumping up and down and she came and turned off the machine. Mr. Haskin was there in a second, demanding to know why Agnes had turned off the machine. When she explained about Smokey, who had jumped down and run away by this time, Mr. Haskin was so furious that the tip of his nose went white. Then he said that cats are a nuisance and Smokey is to be drowned in the river. He said he was going to send a boy with a sack.

When Mr. Haskin left nobody needed to say anything. If Mr. Haskin would drown Smokey, who is almost an operative in this room, then what would he do with kittens? Mrs. Murphy found a basket. Agnes took off her apron. I collected the kittens from the bin. I found Smokey in her usual hiding place. We put them all into the basket. The multicoloured kitten didn't want to go in the basket and she gave me a big scratch on my hand. Then Auntie Janet tied the apron securely around the basket and we hid it in the toilet. We were all hard back at work when Fred from wet finishing arrived with a gunny sack. Mrs. Brown, who is his aunt, told him to go put rocks in the sack and throw it in the river. She was very fierce.

There was a lot of cat complaining from the toilet for the rest of the day. Mr. Haskin did not show his face.

When the closing bell rang Auntie Janet looked at me and said, "Well, are we ready for five cats?"

How did she know, that I so wanted a kitten?

We walked home with Mrs. Campbell and Murdo and Kathleen. I carried the basket of kittens and Kathleen carried Smokey in her pinafore. She was good as gold. When we got to our place we took the cat and kittens around to the back where there is a little tumbledown shed. Murdo found a box and Auntie found an old piece of blanket. I fetched a saucer of milk.

I know that I want that patchwork kitten for my own. Mrs. Campbell says that she will find homes for all the rest because she is used to dealing with large families, but that they must all stay with Smokey for some weeks yet so that she can teach them how to be cats.

When Uncle James got home and heard the story he told us we were scallywags to bring home such a crew, but then went right out back to visit them.

My kitten will need a name. What? I could name him for what he looks like. Or I could give him a people name I like. Or I could name him after something I love. Patch? Adam? Butter?

June 16

Dear Papa and Mama,

I visited the kittens first thing this morning. They have their eyes open and I think the patchwork kitten knows he is mine. He looked right at me. As I watched Smokey giving them their breakfast I thought of the perfect name for him — Mungo. It's a mill name. The barrel that holds the little leftover scraps of cloth is called the mungo barrel and that is just like him, a little leftover bit of a thing that might have been thrown away. I told Murdo on the way to work and he says the name Mungo is too much like his name, but I said that almost everyone can tell the difference between a boy and a kitten so it will likely not be confusing. Then he clenched his hands into paws and licked them and started to wash his face. He is the most comical person I have ever met.

June 17

Dear Papa and Mama,

At dinner I sat with Agnes and she told me one more thing about those commissioners who are coming. A worrying thing. She says they are looking for children who are working when they are too young. She says that girls are supposed to be fourteen years old to work at the mill. She says I am against the law. What must I do?

Mr. Boothroyd did not ask me one thing about how old I was when he took me on. I did not lie. If I tell the inspectors the truth I will likely lose the job. And then I am sure I will have to go back to the Home. I cannot. I just cannot. I will lose heart if I have to leave Auntie and Uncle and Almonte.

I could say that I am fourteen. I am a tall girl for eleven. But I know that you would not care for me to lie.

I cannot tell Auntie. I do not want to burden her. I asked Agnes not to tell her. But what about Ann and the weave room trio? What about Murdo and the other boys?

I thought of the story of the magical cloak. I need to have the wisdom of the fairies, which is older than the beginning of the world, for I don't know what is the right thing to do.

June 18

Dear Papa and Mama,

Payday and I lost ten cents from my pay for being three minutes late on Monday! Auntie said that she does not often agree with Agnes, but she does agree that locking us out when we are just a few minutes late is unfair. I thought that she would not give me twenty cents, but she did anyway so I bought liver for Smokey and a cotton hankie.

The kittens are growing fast. They make very loud noises for such tiny creatures. It is impossible to watch kittens and be downhearted so I have decided to put the commissioners' visit out of my mind. Everything in the town is getting ready for the big Jubilee celebration. I walked by the Agricultural

Grounds this evening and there was a band practising marching and men were building arches over Mill Street.

There is an ongoing story in the newspaper. It is called "The Haunted Hotel" and it is by Mr. Wilkie Collins. It is about a woman called The Countess, who is a European adventuress with a "reputation of the blackest possible colour." Auntie Janet said that perhaps it was not a suitable story for me to read, but Uncle James said that I was a sensible girl and he was sure I would stop as soon as it got unsuitable.

June 19

Dear Papa and Mama,

Today really was a sun day. After church Kathleen and Murdo and I wandered south along the river toward Appleton. We took bread and cheese. We found a shallow place for paddling. Murdo took his fishing rod, but he didn't have luck catching any fish. Kathleen and I made daisy chains and then we looked at clouds. Moon-Shadow, Sundew and Bladderwort can change colours to make themselves invisible. Tree-bark brown, daisy-middle yellow, river green, new-grass green, kingfisher blue, air nothing. That's why you never see them.

Kathleen asked me what I thought of Fred from wet finishing. I said I thought he was kind, and brave to disobey Mr. Haskin about the kittens. Then Murdo began to tease Kathleen, how she was sweet on Fred. I could see that Kathleen wasn't in the mood to be teased so I got Murdo to stop by asking him what wet finishing was. By the time he had finishing telling me how the woven cloth is scoured and soaked and pounded and twisted and rolled between rollers he had forgotten about Fred. Then he wandered off and Kathleen and I had a good talk. She *is* sweet on Fred, but she thinks he isn't sweet on her.

I love being lazy. I love being outside. I love the things there are — birds, trees, clouds, sun, squishy mud between my toes. And I love the things there are not — bells, clocks, machine noise, dust, supervisors, bobbins, ceilings.

I spent the evening embroidering a border on my new hankie. It is not quite beautiful enough to fool the fairies, but almost.

June 20

Dear Papa and Mama,

Tomorrow is the Jubilee! I can hardly wait. There seemed to be more hours in the day today, and more bobbins. I learned another verse of poetry to have something in my head rather than, "How many hours until tomorrow?":

For, like strains of martial music,
Their mighty thoughts suggest
Life's endless toil and endeavour;
And tonight I long for rest.

June 21

Dear Papa and Mama,

Today was a day that I will remember for the rest of my life. It was sublime. If Queen Victoria had been in Almonte she would have been amazed. One of the important men who gave speeches said that nowhere in Canada was the Jubilee celebrated with more loyalty and enthusiasm than in our town of Almonte.

I will try to give you a pencil picture of the day, but even if I were Mr. Wilkie Collins I could not tell you everything.

I woke up early. Auntie and Uncle had a lie-in, but I could not sleep in on such a day. Even by first light the town was crowded with people, all cheerful and dressed in their finest. Some country people from the north came in on the train at three in the morning! The streets were like a place I had never been, a magic place. It dawned bright and sunny and flags were flying from all the buildings, snapping in the wind. Over the street, arches were decorated with greenery and flowers. Chinese lanterns and streamers hung everywhere. I felt as though two eyes were not enough eyes for looking.

Some of the country people asked me for directions and of course I knew where to go and I stood outside myself and looked at myself and thought, "She's an Almonter." I felt proud — of Almonte, and myself and Queen Victoria and the whole British Empire!

At six o'clock in the morning every bell in town began to ring — all the mill bells, and we didn't even have to go there. At the same time there was a gun salute from Bay Hill. All that hubbub must have woken up Auntie and Uncle and all other slugabeds.

I went down to the Agricultural Grounds to see the parade getting ready and there I met up with Murdo. It was grand. Murdo wanted to get close to the steam fire engine. The firemen kept shooing him away, but just in a jolly way. There were masses of school children, mostly dressed in white, carrying little flags. Murdo picked up a flag for me and I was glad to have it to wave for Queen Victoria. When the parade was about to start Murdo suddenly grabbed my arm and dragged me away. He told me he had the best secret place to watch from. We ran through the crowds. A field of people. The best place turned out to be a tree. Murdo gave me a boost up and then I gave him a hand up. There were two very comfortable branches to sit on. Queen Victoria herself could not have had a better view. (But I don't think she climbs trees because Queens probably are not allowed to, and anyway, in the picture in the newspaper she looks like a very plump person.)

Every shining brass instrument in the whole of Lanark County must have been in Almonte that day. From a tree you can see right down into a tuba. There were certainly a lot of strains of martial music. There were banners with gold fringes and tassels. They said *Victoria's Jubilee* and *Canada Our Home* There were satin uniforms and hundreds of school children. Murdo nearly fell out of the tree when the fire engine rolled by, pulled by four huge shiny horses. Horses look very beautiful from a tree as well. There was a wagon with a Singer sewing machine on it and someone was actually sewing as it moved. There was a threshing machine and a binder and a Gatling gun, all being pulled along.

Odd thing. When the steam engine came by I found myself looking around to make sure all the little ones were safe, as though I were still at the Home, and minding them. Then I remembered that I'm not minding anybody except myself.

After the parade there were sports and contests at the Driving Park at the far end of the Agricultural Grounds, and when all the people went that way it was like a flooding river turning in its course. On the way we met up with Auntie Janet and Uncle

James. Uncle James was in a teasing mood and kept saying that he was going to be a rich man later in the day and all because of Her Majesty Queen Victoria and he wouldn't tell us what he meant.

We watched the baseball until the Almonte Evening Stars beat the Carleton Place Mississippis and then Uncle James wanted to go to the cricket. I think cricket is a dull game for the watchers. The only amusing thing was that Auntie Janet noticed that the umpire for the Almonte team was Mr. Flanagan and when she pointed him out to Uncle James he said, "My goodness, he has legs!"

I knew exactly what he meant. Mr. Flanagan seems like a person who only sits at his desk in his office at the mill. We sat on the grass and made daisy chains.

When it came time for the races we found out that Uncle James was going to enter the half-mile foot race, which was open to all. Before he went to the starting line he kissed Auntie Janet, right in front of everybody, and she said, "Run like the wind." There were such a lot of runners that we couldn't see the race for dust and crowds, but Uncle James must have run like the wind because he came in second and won a prize, which was four dollars. Four dollars! In just a few minutes. Auntie Janet said he should give up weaving and become a race runner and Uncle James said, "God bless Queen Victoria!"

In the evening there was a concert with bands and choirs. The whole town was illuminated and it was like fairyland. Uncle bought ice cream for us and all the Campbells with his new wealth. At the end the band played "Rule Britannia" and everyone sang and it was as grand as a speeding train or a great thunderstorm. I couldn't hear myself sing and yet I felt my voice was as big as all Almonte. Then there were fireworks, but I cannot write about one more thing. Uncle James said it was a "Calithumpian good day."

June 22

Dear Papa and Mama,

After the Jubilee everything seems flat. We looked forward to it for so long and now it is over.

Today it rained and all the decorations got soggy and Almonte went from looking like fairyland to looking like any damp place. I wonder if Queen Victoria is feeling a bit let down herself? It must be quite something, knowing that all over the Empire people are having a party for you and then the next day you just go back to work. I'm not quite sure what Queen work is, apart from leading us to a higher plane of civilization. (That's what one of the important men said in a speech.)

Mungo's eyes have changed colour from blue to

green and he has learned to purr. He is the prettiest kitten. I wonder if Queen Victoria is allowed to have a kitten in the palace.

June 24

Dear Papa and Mama,

I am at home even though it is the middle of the day. I had an accident at the mill. I had crawled under the machine to twist a broken thread when a mouse ran over my bare foot. (I take my shoes off to save them.) It startled me so much that I sat up sharply and hit my head hard on the machine. Next thing I knew was Auntie Janet's face close to mine and blood on my pinafore. I knocked myself out under there and the only way they could get me out was to drag me by my feet. My head was bleeding where I cut it and my face was scraped from the floor. The doctor came and bandaged me up. Then Auntie Janet walked me home. I wasn't very steady at walking and I vomited twice in the gutter on the way.

I feel terrible to be such a bother. I know it is not sensible to be scared by a mouse. Mr. Haskin was mean about letting Auntie Janet off to bring me home, even though Agnes said she would mind Auntie Janet's machine.

My head hurts in two different ways. The pain all

over comes in waves and on my face it burns all the time. But mostly I am so sleepy.

June 25

Dear Papa and Mama,

I wanted to go to work today, but when I got up the world was still tipping back and forth. So Auntie made me stay home. Mungo was happy about that.

I have a big lump on my head. Uncle calls it a goose egg. Auntie told me that on the way home yesterday I just kept asking, over and over, "Have I spoiled my pinafore?" I don't remember that at all. The not remembering is frightening. This morning Uncle James collected my pay, which was not very much because of missing two days. Auntie Janet lost two hours for taking care of me yesterday. That made Uncle angry, but she said, "They're not likely to be paying me if I'm not working, James." Auntie and Uncle can disagree about something without getting one bit angry. I wonder if that is another family thing.

Sleepy again.

June 26

Dear Papa and Mama,

My head feels better, but I was still glad to stay in bed this morning. We missed church. Auntie got all the blood stains out of my pinafore.

It is very hot. The outside is as steamy as the inside of the mill.

Auntie and I went for a short walk this afternoon and we saw a poster about a Temperance lecture. It is on Thursday evening. The lecturer is to be Miss Beulah Young. I asked what a lecture is and Auntie says it is like a sermon, but women can do it. I do not think I want to listen to more than one sermon a week, but Auntie seemed excited about going and she would like me to go with her. Uncle James does not want to go.

June 27

Dear Papa and Mama,

Back to work today. There are sweet peas in bloom in a garden on Edward Street, spilling out over the fence. Uncle James picked me a stem and I put it in my buttonhole. The smell made me think of pegging out washing with Alice. Cook planted sweet peas by the back door at the Home. Alice and I often had the job of pegging out the laundry and that sweet pea smell made me remember the weight of wet sheets and the sounds of birds and laughing with Alice.

As soon as Auntie Janet and I got up to the spinning room the noise made my head start to pound again. The sweet peas drooped in the hot, damp air and lost their smell. The first time I had to twist a broken thread, I didn't want to go under the machine. It seemed alive. I didn't want to be a piecer or a doffer girl. I wanted to run down the stairs and out the front door, over the bridge, up Mill Street, along the railway tracks and over the fence into the Edward Street garden where I could hide under a bush and make believe all day.

But I am a mill girl, so I made myself go under the machine. The second time was not so hard.

June 28

Dear Papa and Mama,

Today's bit from the newspaper is the story of how two train car loads of silk came through Almonte last Saturday in the middle of the night. The silk came from Japan and was going to New York City on the C.P.R. That much silk was worth $360,000. Oh how I wish I could have seen it. I had a silk hankie once, as a present at the Home. I asked Uncle James if spinning silk was like spinning wool and he said that silk is spun by worms! I thought he was having a joke, but it turns out to be true. Then we all thought of all the spinners at the mill being giant worms. Especially Mr. Haskin. A skinny worm. I will never forget when he was going to drown Smokey.

The kittens are growing like billy-oh. They try to walk, but they keep falling over their own paws. Mrs. Campbell, who knows all about kittens, says that in three weeks they can leave their mother. I can't wait to move Mungo from the shed to my snug.

Oh. I just thought of something. What will Mr. Haskin do when Smokey appears back at the mill?

The cut on my head has turned into a scab and it is very itchy.

June 29

Dear Papa and Mama,

It is too hot to sleep. We sit out on the front steps in the dark and so does everybody else, up and down the road.

June 30

Dear Papa and Mama,

Tonight was the Temperance lecture. The town hall was very full. I saw several people from church there, and from the mill — more women than men. First of all a young man came on the stage and sang a very rousing song that went, "Speed thee on, the cause of Temperance, Raise the Temperance banner high."

Then Miss Beulah Young came on the stage. She

is beautiful. She had on a lovely suit and she was very neat, but the best thing was her voice. She had a way of speaking that is like the Bible. She did not seem to be speaking loudly, but her voice filled the whole hall.

The title of the lecture was "Will Your Anchor Hold?" It was all about the wickedness of drinking, how alcohol makes people poor and sick and how it makes families unhappy. Miss Beulah Young is a member of the Women's Christian Temperance Union and they think that alcohol should not be allowed at all.

Another thing that is not like a sermon is that Miss Young told us all about herself. She told us about her childhood, how her mother died when she was very young and how she cared for her sick father and how she had a message from God that she had a mission, not in foreign lands, but right here, in taverns and saloons. She told us many sad stories about men who drank and ruined themselves and their wives and children. She asked if we would stand by and watch while a man was given poison — and yet that is just what we do when we stand by and watch as millionaires make money selling alcohol.

She said we must band together. She said that a human being is like a ship, on a long voyage from childhood. There will be calm seas and storms, arctic winds and warm tropical breezes. If we set our sails wisely no storm can drive us off our track. The winds of change will bring us even faster toward our goal. And as we pass other ships we can hoist signals of goodwill and helpfulness. But if we set our sails foolishly, by drinking, the winds of trial and change will drive us to the rocks of despair.

Everything she said was like that. You could see a picture of it in your mind. (Especially the picture of arctic winds. The town hall full of people was hotter than hot and we would have welcomed a bit of arctic wind.)

Then she handed out little slips of paper. Printed on the slips was a promise never to drink alcohol. You can sign the slip and put it in the collection plate. "Promise by promise," she said, "we can change the world." I was happy to sign my slip and so was Auntie Janet. I never thought before that I could be part of changing the world.

(Now that I am home I have remembered that I never wanted to drink alcohol anyway. I've never tasted it, but when you walk by the tavern and breathe in, it smells disgusting. So signing the promise was not really noble of me, although when I did it I felt rather noble, just for a moment.)

The lecture ended with a song, rather like a hymn. Auntie Janet and I could not get it out of our heads and we sang it softly on the way home.

Drops in an ocean of infinite might;
We all belong, we all belong;
Rays in a prism of white radiant light;
We all belong, we all belong.
Strands in a cord reaching down from God's throne,
Links in a chain which now circles each zone,
Notes in the deepest of harmonies known;
We all belong, we all belong.

I remembered how I felt on Jubilee day, like something bigger than myself.

When we passed by the tavern I imagined myself going in and telling all the men about setting their sails wisely and getting them to sign the pledge. I wish I could speak like Miss Beulah Young.

July 1

Dear Papa and Mama,

Happy Dominion Day to Canada, which is twenty years old, the same age as Agnes. Something is up with Agnes. Fred, from wet finishing, seems to be finding lots of reasons to visit the spinning room. He comes up and asks if anything wants doing, but really I think he is courting Agnes. He often joins us for the dinner break. Agnes does not appear to favour him. When the other women tease her she flips her hair and says, "I'm certainly setting my sights higher than Fred Armstrong, if I'm setting my sights at all, which I am not." Today he brought her a stick of apple blossom in a jam jar. I am sorry for Kathleen.

July 4

Dear Papa and Mama,

Last night just after supper we had a grand storm. When we got off work this evening the outside was so steamy and hot that it felt as though you could wring the air like laundry. Then later a huge black cloud appeared and there was thunder and lightning and the rain fell in buckets as though someone was throwing it against the windows. The house rattled with the wind. Uncle James started saying verses from the Psalms. "The voice of thy thunder was in the heaven, the lightnings lightened the world; the earth trembled and shook." Auntie Janet said he should become a preacher. He said he would rather go on the stage.

In the gap between the thunder and the lightning I heard your voice, Papa, counting off the seconds. Laird howling and you counting and holding me tight. That gap is magic. I always think that I might see a fairy. But I never have.

July 5

Dear Papa and Mama,

Somebody in the weaving room heard that an

entire barn out toward Carp was blown over in the storm. The animals were rescued in time.

The storm left everything hotter and wetter than ever, especially inside the mill. Walking home today I felt like a piece of cabbage that had been boiled for hours. We passed by two of those skipping girls, sitting on a porch, chatting and sipping and waving paper fans. They did not look like cabbage. Now that school is over I wonder how they spend their days. Every day must be like Sunday to them. I know — Commandment number ten: Thou shalt not covet any thing that is thy neighbour's.

July 6

Dear Papa and Mama,

We found out today that the commissioners will come next month. I had stored this worry away, but now it is back. At dinnertime everyone was talking about it, but nobody talked about the age question, thank goodness. I still do not know what to do.

July 8

Dear Papa and Mama,

Tonight in the newspaper there was something about a strike in the cotton mill at Cornwall. The mill owner lowered the workers' wages. Uncle James explained about strikes. It is when the workers won't work any more until the owners give them what they want. Auntie Janet said that strikes are wicked and Uncle James said that they are the only thing to do when wealthy employers treat the workers as if they were slaves. And then Auntie Janet said that Mr. Flanagan does not treat us like slaves. She said that Uncle James should remember how we had a holiday for the Jubilee and that the Almonte mill pays more than the other mills and we have a garden and everything.

Who is right? I hate it when I don't know what is the right thing to think. I went out to the shed to tell my worries to Mungo. He now has teeth and Smokey is getting a bit grumpy about feeding him and the other kittens. Mrs. Campbell says we must start to bring scraps for them.

The story by Mr. Wilkie Collins is getting more and more mysterious. Why is the Countess Narona visiting the frank and simple Miss Lockwood? She is up to no good.

July 9

Dear Papa and Mama,

More worries. There was more in the newspaper about the strike in Cornwall. I did not read it aloud to Auntie and Uncle. A minister who was supporting the strikers said that they should report how many underage children were working at the mill because the Ontario Factories Act says that they must not, and those children are taking the place of other people who would have to be paid more money. I don't understand this. A grown woman could not do my job because she would be too big to crawl under to mend the broken threads. And of course children do not earn what adults earn. They are smaller and weaker. That is like saying that women should earn the same as men. But if a minister thinks this is right and ministers are clever and good, how can I disagree? None of these thoughts makes it any easier to decide if I should tell the truth when the commissioners come. And now I feel that I'm keeping a secret from Auntie and Uncle. I don't think they know about the Ontario Factories Act. What would you do, Mama and Papa?

July 11

Dear Papa and Mama,

Agnes, who always seems to know things, says that the commissioners are coming the week of August 8. This is too many weeks to worry what I will do. Maybe they will not really come. Maybe the rules will change by then. Maybe I will have a revelation and a sign, like people in the Bible.

July 13

Dear Papa and Mama,

A mystery. What does Uncle James want with a ball of yellow wool? Auntie Janet won't give it to him until he tells her what it is for, but he won't. It is a standoff. Do you think he is taking up knitting? I have given up on my socks for now. Nobody sensible wants to knit in this hot weather.

July 16

Dear Papa and Mama,

Payday. We bought ice cream as a treat.

July 17

Dear Papa and Mama,

The lesson at church today was about the children of Israel living for forty years in the wilderness with just manna to eat. If I had to eat just one thing for forty years I would choose ice cream.

This afternoon I went down to the river with Murdo and Kathleen. We paddled and made stick-and-leaf boats and raced them. I wish I didn't have to go to work tomorrow. There. I have said it. I would never tell Auntie and Uncle, but Sundays are so pleasant. Time on Sundays flies like a fairy. Time at the mill creeps.

July 19

Dear Papa and Mama,

I saw a poster today on the side of the bank building for a circus that is coming to Almonte. It had a picture of a beautiful lady flying through the air. It is called the Frank Robbins Circus and it says it is the "largest, grandest, and best amusement institution in all the world." Admission is ten cents. I have that much money saved up, but how can we go when we are at work every day except Sunday and they won't have a circus on a Sunday? The skipping girls will be free to go any time, as they have every day of the summer to call their own.

July 21

Dear Papa and Mama,

Today I got to visit the dye shed. Murdo took me round at dinner. To get there we had to go through the wool sorting room. Mr. Houghton is the chief wool sorter. He is an important man, but kindly. He took a fleece and showed me which parts were good for what kind of yarn. "It's a matter of staple and fibre and feel," he said. "See this? Feel it. Shoulder, now that will make a lovely worsted yarn. Some banker will be wearing that some day. Sides and back, likely good for woollens. Flanks, good for blankets." Murdo says that that is the only part of mill work that can never be done by machine, because the wool sorters have to look at every fleece and decide which parts go where. "Aye," said Mr. Houghton, "until machines can think or we all dress in furs there will always be wool sorters."

When we left, Murdo told me that Mr. Houghton usually says, "Until machines can think or we all go naked," but he was being more proper with me.

The next room was mysterious. All the walls were painted black. Murdo says this is because if the walls were any colour at all, even white, it would reflect the light and the true colour of the cloth could not be judged.

Then we came to the room with the huge vats of dye. They are like a witch's cauldron for giant witches. Across the top are walkways and I imagined somebody falling in. I scared myself imagining it. Once you've had this kind of thought it is hard to unthink it. I told Murdo, but he just asked me if I would like to be indigo blue or cochineal red. Then he showed me the dyes, which have lovely names. Madder, cochineal, indigo, gambier, sumac, nutgall. He told me you can make dye from any part of a plant — berries, flowers and leaves — and also from insects, which is what cochineal is. I asked if madder was red and he said it was! Indigo and Gambier would make splendid names for fairies.

July 22

Dear Papa and Mama,

Why are mosquitoes so fond of me? I have twenty-six bites. I might have more because I think some of the new bites are on top of the old bites. I try not to scratch. Maybe mosquitoes are bad fairies in disguise.

Lord Montbarry, husband of the Countess Narona, has died in Venice. Turns out that Miss Lockwood was engaged to Lord Montbarry before he married the Countess. "Ah-ha," says Uncle, "it is all coming clear." Not to me.

July 23

Dear Papa and Mama,

You will be surprised to know that today your daughter became a minister. Perhaps you did not know that girls could be ministers, but that is because you have never been to the Almonte Woollen Mill No. 1. When we all arrived this morning there was a lot of laughing and carrying on among the men, especially the men from the dye room. We didn't know what it was about until the dinner hour. Fred Armstrong came up and said we should come down to the garden, as we were needed. He had a great grin on his face. First thing I saw when I got there was Murdo's father in a dress! He had a veil over his head and there were flowers tucked into it. It looked so comical, his great red beard sticking out from under the veil. Then I saw Uncle James wearing a yellow wool wig! (Mystery solved!) It turns out that Mr. Stafford, the overseer of the fulling room, is going to be married, so all the hands in the mill decided to have a mock wedding.

At this wedding everyone was opposite. The bride was Murdo's father, the bridesmaid was Uncle James, the groom was Mrs. Easton, who is a tiny woman from the weaving room. She had a top hat that was so big that it kept falling right down over her eyes and resting on her nose. All the women were dressed as men and all the men as women.

The other opposite thing was that all the young people pretended to be old. One of the sweepers, Willie, had a pillow tucked into his shirt and a make-believe pocket watch and he was pretending to be the mill owner. And then they asked me to be the minister and marry the couple! I put on a dark jacket and a piece of white paper around my neck for a clerical collar. The bride and groom walked up the aisle while somebody played a mouth organ.

At first I was bashful because I didn't know what words to say. I have never been to a wedding. But I didn't really have to say anything because everyone kept calling out things that the groom had to promise. They made him promise to wash all the dishes and cook all the meals and change the baby's nappies! Mrs. Easton has a very big voice for a very small woman and she kept promising everything and then all the women cheered and all the men groaned. Then I had to say (Auntie Janet whispered it to me), "I pronounce you man and wife," and then Mrs. Easton kissed Murdo's father (through the veil) and then everybody cheered and threw bits of cut-up paper for confetti.

Then a large box was presented to the married couple. It was tied up with ribbon. As they were opening it Agnes kept saying things like, "Oh, I do wonder if it is going to be a silver teapot?" and "Do you think it is a cut-crystal rose bowl?" Well, it was a chamber pot! Then everyone went back to being themselves and went back to work. Men as men, women as women, Flora as Flora.

July 24

Dear Papa and Mama,

At church today I had a funny thought. As Rev. Parfitt was taking the service I felt as though I could do it. Even though the mock wedding yesterday was all a joke, a play got up for fun, I still felt as though I had been a real minister for a minute or two. It made me think how grand that would be, to help people out in their troubles and to share in their joys, to stand up in front of everyone and proclaim a blessing over them.

July 25

Dear Papa and Mama,

Two exciting things to write about today. The first is that Mungo has moved in. The Campbells are keeping the grey kitten and Mrs. Campbell has found homes for the two tabbies. As to the question of what to do with Smokey, Mrs. Campbell says we will just take her back to the mill. Auntie Janet asked what about Mr. Haskin and Mrs. Campbell looked fierce and said, "Leave that Mr. Haskin to me." Mungo settled right into my snug. He likes to ride on my shoulder and lick my nose.

The second exciting things is that we can go to the circus after all! On Saturday Mr. Flanagan will close the mill one hour early so that we can all go. Why isn't it Saturday today! Thank goodness for sleeping when you don't have to wait for time to pass.

July 26

Dear Papa and Mama,

Murdo told me a very sad story. A few years ago an elephant named Jumbo broke away from the circus and ran across the railway track just as a train was coming and he was killed. The circus people and animals must have felt that they lost a friend. I wonder if there will be elephants at this circus.

Smokey is back at the mill, in the spinning room. Mr. Haskin must have noticed her, but he is pretending that he hasn't.

July 27

Dear Papa and Mama,

Bad news about the circus. Murdo cannot go, as the Campbells cannot manage the admission. I asked Auntie Janet if we could pay for Murdo and she said that she had already offered, but Murdo refused, because of pride. Also, would Murdo want to go if his parents and Kathleen and his middle brother Percy could not go as well? (The others are too small to care about a circus.) She is right. He wouldn't.

July 28

Dear Papa and Mama,

The best thing has happened. Last night when we were walking home from the mill, Murdo found a shiny fifty-cent piece on the path. Now the Campbells can go to the circus! Auntie and Uncle were so happy. "Pays to watch your feet," said Uncle.

A little later

Dear Papa and Mama,

I just figured something out, I think. I was thinking again about the luck of Murdo finding a fifty-cent piece and then I remembered that just before he found it, Uncle (who was walking ahead of us) stopped to tie his boots. I think he left the coin for Murdo to find. I cannot be sure, but it would be like him. He knows how to be kind and still let somebody be proud.

July 30

Dear Papa and Mama,

Circus day. I think there is more to remember in this day than any day of my life so far.

It all started when the circus train arrived very early in the morning. I got up and dressed at the crack of dawn and collected Murdo and we were at the station to see it arrive. It was more than twenty cars long, all very clean and shipshape. I remembered my train trip to Almonte. Oh, I would love to live in a train, click-clacking through the night, waking up in a new place every day.

First they unloaded the tents and we followed the circus people over to the Agricultural Grounds to see them unpack them and put them up. But then somebody said, "Here come the elephants!" so we raced back to the train in time to see a line of elephants walking down a ramp. I have never seen such a sight. Six altogether. They are bigger in real life than they look on the poster. They look gentle, for something so big. Murdo says I would change my mind on that if I was in the path of a herd of them thundering through the jungle toward me. "You would need an elephant gun," he said. Why are boys so horrid, always thinking about killing things?

As the elephants started to walk, in a long line, the dust rose up from their huge feet and the morning sun was shining through the dust and it was like a scene from a magic land. A mean circus man tried to shoo us away, but Murdo and I know all the places to hide around the station so we got to see it all. Then we had to run like billy-oh to be at work on time. The hours from seven to eleven crept by so slowly. Bobbins have never been so tiresome.

When the bell rang we scooted back to the Agricultural Grounds. The tents were already up, making a town right there by the river. Beautiful red-and-white striped tents with flags and banners flying. By then there were many more people around and more mean circus men and they got a fence built in a big hurry. So that was it for the morning, but we had the show to look forward to.

To describe the circus show would take a whole pencil right down to a nub and another day's holiday. There was a huge crowd. I think everyone from Almonte was there and lots of country people as well. We sat right behind the Campbells. Percy was so excited that he kept jumping up and Mr. Campbell kept pushing him down like a jack-in-the-box.

I will just tell you about my favourite act: Charles Fish, Hero Horseman of the Universe. I got the feeling it was going to be amazing when Mr. Fish got on the horse by running toward it and jumping up on its back, landing squarely on his two feet. Then the horse started to run in a circle around the ring and Mr. Fish just stayed there, bareback, nothing to hold onto, looking as ordinary as someone standing on a street corner. That was amazing enough, but then he started to do somersaults, backwards and forwards. Then he stood on one foot and spun around, like a top. Then two fancy circus ladies came out and stood on stools, holding up a big paper disc. Mr. Fish stood on the horse, the horse ran toward the disc and under it while Mr. Fish did a dive *through* the disc and then a somersault in the air and landed on the horse's back again. There was a little pause while everyone was thinking, "Did I just see that?" and then everybody started to stamp and clap and whistle. So then the fancy circus ladies got another disc and he did the same thing, but backwards!

The elephants did a ballet. Most people laughed,

but it didn't strike me that way. I just got this feeling of amazement that there should be such creatures on earth. The clowns pretended to be firefighters and rescued a very fat lady (really a clown with padding) from a burning building. They tried to make her jump into a blanket that they were holding by the edges, but she wouldn't so then they got ladders, but the ladders kept collapsing and Uncle James laughed so hard he snorted through his nose. There were lions, miniature horses, high-wire acrobats and minstrels, but I cannot describe them all.

As we walked home Murdo said that he wanted to run away with the circus when they left Almonte. And then we decided that we would all like to run away. Uncle James wants to be an elephant trainer. Auntie Janet said she wants to be a clown. I'd like to learn to be a bareback equestrian and Murdo can't decide between an acrobat, the trumpet-playing minstrel or the man at the door who collects all the money.

July 31

Dear Papa and Mama,

On the way to church we saw the circus people taking down the circus tent. It rained in the night and the ground was muddy. The people looked ordinary and a bit grubby. No sign of the elephants. But still, all day I kept thinking about going away on the train with them all, chugging along to the next town. But of course I would have to take Auntie and Uncle, and Murdo and Mungo, and Murdo would have to take his family, and soon the whole town of Almonte would be moving! But we wouldn't let Mr. Haskin come.

August 1

Dear Papa and Mama,

It was tedious at the mill today. Endless toil and endeavour. I memorized the next bit of "The Day is Done":

Read from some humbler poet,
Whose songs gushed from his heart,
As showers from the clouds of summer,
Or tears from the eyelids start.

I wonder if Mr. Longfellow wrote this in summer? It is so hot that I wish for some showers from the clouds of summer. I also wish I could wear spangles and ride bareback.

August 2

Dear Papa and Mama,

Auntie Janet says we're having "dog days." She just

means that it is still very hot. I don't know why you would call them dog days because dogs don't like it. Barney's yellow dog just lies in the shade and pants. The only person who is not flattened by the heat is Mungo, who is as lively as ever, so I think we should call them "cat days." Here are some things about him:

He loves to chase scrunched-up paper balls.
His favourite thing is to hide in the woodbox.
He continues to grow and his tail is longer and wavy-er.
He licks my nose in the morning if I don't open my eyes right away.

August 3

Dear Papa and Mama,

The only place to be is near the river. After work today, Murdo, Kathleen, Auntie and I did not even go home. We just went straight along the river to our favourite place.

It is shady and the sound of the water makes you feel a bit cooler. We sat with our feet in the water and Auntie told a story. It's called "The lass who went out at the cry of dawn." A girl goes out at dawn to wash her face in the dew to make herself prettier and she disappears. Her younger sister goes on a journey to look for her. Her mother gives her a package of yarn, a needle, pins and a silver thimble. She hears about a wicked wizard, who lives in a castle on Mischanter Hill, who steals away young girls. On the way to the castle she meets a tinker and a ragged beggar and she is kind to them and they give her magic advice. The tinker says, "What you see and hear are not what they seem to be." The beggar says, "Gold and silver are a match for evil." When the sister arrives at the wizard's castle he invites her in and then he puts her to many tests, like fire and a vicious wolf, but she is brave and clever and she rescues her sister, and vanquishes the wizard using magic and her sewing things. On the way home they meet two fine young men and it turns out that they are the tinker and the beggar, who were under the wizard's wicked spell. And they fall in love and marry them and live happily all the rest of their days.

Auntie Janet said that when she heard the story from her granny she thought it meant that you should always carry a thimble. And then Kathleen said that the story means that if she is stolen away then Murdo has to come and rescue her because that is his duty as a brother. And then Murdo said that the story means that Kathleen should go out in the morning and wash her face in the dew so that she will become better looking and someone will want to marry her. And then Kathleen picked up

Murdo and threw him right into the river! He bobbed up snorting and laughing and then he tried to splash us all, but we beat a retreat.

I didn't say what I thought of the story because (secret) it made me a bit sad. I am so lucky to have Auntie Janet and Uncle James as my family, but when I heard about that loyal sister, and sometimes when I see how Murdo is with Kathleen and Percy and the little ones, I long for a brother or a sister.

August 4

Dear Papa and Mama,

This afternoon I saw something so sad that I am almost afraid to write it down. It will make me cry. I was walking along Mill Street. Barney was sitting outside the livery stable as usual, with his yellow dog. He wasn't yelling or glaring at anybody, but just sort of slumped over. There were two high-school boys passing in front of him, throwing a baseball from one to the other. Suddenly one of them threw the baseball really hard at Barney's head, calling out "Catch!" and laughing in the meanest way. Barney reached up with his stump of an arm and the ball whizzed right by his ear. Then he started to yell. The boys just ran away. I was afraid so I hurried on by. But I was full of anger. Why am I just a girl? I wanted to be big and strong, like a policeman, and grab those two boys and bang their heads together and hurt them and make them apologize to Barney.

Here is the worst thing. I could not help seeing the end of Barney's cut-off arm when he reached up and his sleeve fell back. It was pink and wrinkled. I cannot get that picture out of my mind. I do not want to think about this any more.

August 5

Dear Papa and Mama,

Bad dream last night. Creeping things, monsters with many teeth, like wolves, but like machines too. I woke up and then it was so hot that I could not get to sleep again. I used to have many bad dreams at the Home, but not so often since I came to Almonte. I hope they don't start again.

August 7

Dear Papa and Mama,

There is nothing to be said about these dog days except that I think they should be called Bladderwort days. In the newspaper it says that you can revive someone who has had sunstroke by using ammonia. The butcher has a new cooler for his meat. I would not mind being a roast or a chop just long enough to get cooled off.

August 8

Dear Papa and Mama,

Today after work we went out to the Agricultural Grounds to see Uncle James and Mr. Campbell play baseball. I find baseball almost as dull as cricket so I was glad that Granny Whitall came with us. She remembers a lot of things that happened in Almonte and she tells good stories. She told us about a lady balloonist who came to those very fields. Her name was Miss Nellie Thurston, from Oswego, New York. "There were posters all around the town," said Granny Whitall, "and we were all keen to go. Mr. Flanagan closed the mill for the afternoon, and we all went out to Mr. McFarlane's field to see it."

Miss Nellie Thurston got up in her balloon with no problem and sailed for nearly an hour before she came down in Merrickville. That's thirty-five miles away. I tried to imagine it. Would it be like being a bird? Or perhaps a fairy?

"First woman to go up in a balloon in all of Canada," said Granny Whitall, "and it happened right here in Almonte. That's something to be proud of."

Then Murdo said that he remembered seeing it, but Granny Whitall said to him, "Don't be daft. You were just a wee boy at the time."

Then we all talked about the first thing we could

remember. Murdo stuck to his guns and said it was a huge balloon in the sky. I think I remember your beard, Papa. It tickled my nose.

August 9

Dear Papa and Mama,

The commissioners' visit is getting close. Just this morning Auntie said that we would have to let down the hem of my dress, as I have grown since I came to Almonte. This gave me hope that the commissioners would think I was fourteen, but what if they ask? I decided to talk it over with Murdo. He didn't think but a second. "I'll lie," he said. "Otherwise I might be let go. All the lads will lie." I wish it seemed this simple to me.

August 10

Dear Papa and Mama,

The commissioners' visit is getting more and more complicated. Today I talked to the weave room trio. They agree with Murdo. So then I decided that I would tell a lie, that it was the only way. But then I started to worry about Ann. Even if she could remember to lie properly, she is so small that nobody would believe her. The worst thing is that I cannot go to Auntie and Uncle with this problem.

August 11

Dear Papa and Mama,

Today I sat with Agnes at dinner and asked for her help. She understood right away about the lying problem and the Ann problem. Finally she said, "Leave it to me."

August 12

Dear Papa and Mama,

My heart is light. Agnes has come up with a plan for the commissioners' visit. I will not write it down here, but it means that I will not have to lie and I will not get Auntie Janet into trouble and I will not lose my job. It was not actually Agnes who invented this plan, but Fred from wet finishing. Fred is definitely sweet on Agnes. I still cannot tell if Agnes is sweet back on Fred. She mocks him a good deal, but with a twinkle in her eye. This is all very complicated. Sometimes it seems to me a kind of miracle that two people are ever sweet on each other at the same time and in the same place.

I walked home with Ann and told her over and over what she must do.

August 13

Dear Papa and Mama,

Success! I am still a doffer girl at the Almonte

Woollen Mill No. 1. Here is what happened.

First thing this morning, Mr. Haskin made the big announcement that the commissioners were coming. He didn't know that we already knew about it. His nose was even thinner and whiter than usual. Agnes looked over at me and winked.

All morning we waited and I was nervous as can be. Every time somebody came into the room I almost jumped out of my skin. Then we had dinner. Agnes and I went over the details of our plan.

Shortly after we came back from dinner Fred popped his head into the spinning room and gave one of those loud whistles that some men and boys can do by putting two fingers in their mouths. (I have often tried to learn this, but I can only whistle softly in the usual way, without fingers.) That was the signal we had arranged to say that the commissioners were on their way. Mr. Haskin made the popping noise he makes when he is cross and he went to chase Fred away, but he had already disappeared. In the meantime, Agnes left her machine and ran across to the wool storage bin. She leaned over, making her back into a step.

I grabbed Ann's hand and raced over to the bin. But then she stopped dead in her tracks. I told her to climb in but she couldn't seem to hear me. Then Mrs. Brown's voice boomed out. "Ann Smith, into the bin with you this minute." Ann looked terrified and then dived into the bin headfirst. I followed on her heels. As I jumped I caught sight of Auntie Janet. Her eyes were wide as saucers.

As I lay in the wool I couldn't hear a thing and I started to worry. What if Ann gave the game away? What if Mr. Haskin gave the game away? What if Auntie Janet gave the game away? Should we have told her about the plan? Would she be angry? Any minute I expected to see a commissioner's face over the side of the bin.

But nothing of the sort happened. The clatter went on, wool floated in the air. Ann huddled in the corner with her eyes closed. I almost dozed off. Finally, after a good long time, a face did appear over the side of the bin. It was Auntie Janet. She was shaking her head in a chiding sort of way, but she was smiling all the same. She hauled me out and all the spinners applauded and laughed. For the first time ever I saw Ann smile. Mr. Haskin was nowhere to be seen. Agnes said, "You've lost an hour's work, you girls, but I don't think Mr. Haskin is going to mention it."

After work I asked Agnes if she had actually talked to the commissioners about the toilets and she said she had. "I also told them that when we have to eat our dinners indoors in bad weather our food gets dusty. I thought Mr. Haskin was going to explode, but I did it anyway. The commissioners wrote it all down. They were very respectful." I asked her if they had written down her name and she said yes. "Some of the operatives did not want to give their names," she said, "but I'm proud to think of my name written down in a report and read by important people, maybe even far in the future." I thought about Mr. Longfellow's poem and distant footsteps echoing through the corridors of Time.

August 14

Dear Papa and Mama,

This morning Auntie Janet and Uncle James and I had a talk. She had told Uncle James about me hiding in the storage bin. He said that he thought it was clever what I did, but that he wanted to tell me that he hoped that I would not always have to work in the mill. I wanted to say that I did not care to go to school and that I was perfectly happy working. And the first part is the complete truth. I've walked by the school and I know what it would be like there. The girls would mock me. And why do I need to go to school? I already know how to read and write and even do sums.

The second part was not completely true because some days I do not want to go to work. But I don't want to go to school instead! It is just that some days I want to just loaf around, or play. I would like to sit by the river and read, or go on outings, or ride around in a carriage, or spend the day drinking tea from a beautiful china cup and chatting and doing a little embroidery. But that is like saying that I would like to be a princess.

I did not get a chance to say any of this. Uncle had more to say. About the future. He said that there was a very good chance that he could get a job as a loom fixer, maybe next year.

"He's been helping out Mr. Docharty," said Auntie Janet. "Mr. Docharty says he's a very quick study." Auntie Janet sounded very proud when she said this and I knew why. The loom fixer is the most important job in the mill (well, except for supervisors and that). Sometimes when the operatives pass Mr. Docharty on the street they tip their hats.

And there was more. Auntie Janet said that Mr. Haskin had said that she might be able to train for a room girl in the weave room. A room girl supervises all the weaving and she's the person you call on when there is a stoppage in the loom, when the yarn or warp breaks. Then it was Uncle James's turn to look proud. "You'd be a great improvement on that Bessie Murphy, that's for sure." This must be part of being in a family, feeling part of someone else doing well.

"Then you wouldn't have to work," Auntie Janet said to me. "We would earn enough for the three of us and then you could go to school and then you could go to high school and learn to be really clever and then you could do something really grand, like train to be a teacher."

A teacher! No! That would be the Home all over again. Being in charge. Trying to make people do things they didn't want to do. I felt as if I were in the middle of a river and a strong current was pushing me toward the rest of my life.

All I could say was, "Do I have to be a teacher?"

Then they both laughed and Auntie said that I could be anything I wanted. And then Uncle James got silly and said I could be a lady hot-air balloonist or a lady prime minister. I didn't say anything about being a princess.

August 18

Dear Papa and Mama,

Mr. Longfellow is still thinking about the humbler poet.

Who, through long days of labour,
And nights devoid of ease,
Still heard in his soul the music
Of wonderful melodies.

I wonder what the days of labour were? Maybe in a mill? And the nights devoid of ease? It makes me think of bad dreams. I don't tell Auntie or Uncle, but it is as though those machine teeth are waiting for me every night. In the day it is far far back in my mind, but I wish I had never seen Barney's arm with its awful pinkness.

I must not be downhearted. Now that I have eight verses of this poem by heart I can say it over and over again to the background of the spinning machine.

August 21

Dear Papa and Mama,

Today we had a great bee. Mrs. Murphy has a brother-in-law with a farm out Carp way and he brought in several baskets of apples. So she invited us to make applesauce with her. It was hot work, but a good job for three. One cored and trimmed. One minded the sauce kettle and one minded the canning kettle. The apples were rosy and we left the skins on while we sauced them, so the applesauce was a golden pink.

Mrs. Murphy is quiet at work, but a comical person at home. She seems to have a life of many trials, but she makes them all into funny stories. One of her stories was about the time she was attacked by a turkey. She was coming out of church, wearing a new hat with red ribbons. Seems that the minister had a very ill-tempered turkey that he kept penned up, but that morning it escaped. Mrs. Murphy said, "One minute I'm standing making polite Sunday conversation and the next minute this huge gobbler, every feather bristling with rage, is coming right at my head." The turkey knocked off the hat and then when Mrs. Murphy went to pick it up, it flew at her again and knocked her right over. Then she tried to fight it off with her parasol. Then Mr. Houghton ("twice as old as Methuselah, but very gallant") came to her rescue, but as he tried to pull her up, the turkey turned its attention to him and he ended up falling down as well. "Then the turkey, delighted with a double victory, proceeded to walk all over us, pecking."

The way Mrs. Murphy told the story it was like you were there. We nearly burnt a batch of applesauce, we were laughing so hard. Then later, in the middle of another conversation altogether, she said, in a sad sort of way, "I don't know why that turkey objected so strongly to my hat. I thought it was a very nice one," and that set Auntie and me off again.

The second-best moment of making applesauce is when you peek in the pot and all the apple pieces have exploded, like flowers coming into bloom. The first-best moment of applesauce making is when you are done and all the jars are lined up and you wash the stickiness off your hands and sit and have a cup of tea and a dish of warm applesauce. Then you feel happy and virtuous — two feelings that do not always go together, no matter what they say in church.

Before we went home we sat on the front step to catch the evening breeze. In the distance there was the sound of a band practising but Mrs. Murphy could not hear it.

"Left my hearing at the mill," she said, "like all the hands. Ten years of that racket and you lose the small sounds. Funny, it's not the birds I miss so much as the peepers. That little froggy squeaking sound always meant spring to me."

I said that was sad but she just said, "Ah, well. It's a noisy place, the mill. There's no help for that."

August 25

Dear Papa and Mama,

Ever since the commissioners came something has been different at the mill. I can't quite say what, except that it feels like a thunderstorm is about to happen. Today it rained. "Showers from the clouds of summer," as Mr. Longfellow would say. So we all stayed in to eat our dinners. Rain was lashing against the windows and Agnes said, "Look at that grey misery. Let's have a treat. I'll give you a song." Agnes is such a jolly person and she has a grand big voice. She just opens her mouth and out it comes. So she sang us a comic song about a man with a runaway pig.

It was like we had laughter just bottled up inside us and it came gushing out, like water over a mill-race. We were all laughing (well, except Ann, who hasn't a laugh in her anywhere) when Mr. Haskin came in. He said something, but we didn't hear him because the ends of laughing were still in us. So then he tried to clap to get us to be quiet, but his hands just went right by each other. This happens to me when I try to catch a ball and don't. Anyway, I know this is naughty, but then we really could not control our laughter. Mr. Haskin turned bright red and said in a stern way, "There is to be no laughing in the spinning room!"

We all went quiet after that. Then Agnes said, "But sir, are we not allowed to laugh in our dinner hour?"

Mr. Haskin just sputtered like a too-full teakettle and repeated himself. "There is to be no laughing in the spinning room." Then he turned to go and that's when Agnes started clapping, very slowly. I don't know why this was so shocking, but it was.

Mr. Haskin just stood and stared at Agnes, and she stared right back and kept clapping. Mr. Haskin looked like the mean ginger dog on Albert Street, who stares at you and growls. Instead of growling he said, "Miss Bamford, this is a gross impertinence." Then he whirled around and left.

I don't know about the others, but I felt as though I'd had the stuffing knocked out of me. Not Agnes though. She just tossed her head and said, "What we do in our dinner hour is not the business of Mr. Haskin. Back to work, girls!"

Auntie Janet says that Agnes Bamford should watch herself and look to her job. But I couldn't help thinking that in the Bible it says that there is a time to weep and a time to laugh and isn't our dinner hour a time to laugh? But perhaps this is impertinent, even to think.

August 26

Dear Papa and Mama,

This morning, right after we started work, Mr. Haskin said that Agnes was to turn off her machine and come with him to the office. She did not return. Nobody knows why. When Mr. Haskin came back he said that Auntie Janet was to run Agnes's machine as well as her own.

Auntie was very tired at the end of the day. I tried to help with chores more than usual.

August 27

Dear Papa and Mama,

Something must be really wrong because Agnes was not at work again today and it is payday. How will she manage without collecting her pay? Murdo and I walked by her house on the way home from work, but we did not see anybody to ask.

August 28

Dear Papa and Mama,

Today Kathleen and I went blackberry picking. She knows the best places. We picked and ate and picked and ate and ate and ate and ate. Then Auntie made a summer pudding. You take slices of bread and line a pudding basin. Then you fill it with blackberries and put a plate on top and a heavy pot on top of the plate. When you turn it out the blackberry juice has soaked into the bread and it is a lovely purple colour. We ate it for supper with some top cream. If Cook at the Home knew about summer pudding, she kept it a secret.

August 29

Dear Papa and Mama,

This morning Mr. Haskin told us that Agnes is not working for the mill any more. He did not even have the courage to say that she had lost her job until Mrs. Brown came right out and asked him. Then he admitted it and then he disappeared for the rest of the morning.

At dinnertime everyone, from all the parts of the

mill, was talking about it. People were angry. They said it was unfair. Some of the women said what a good spinner Agnes was. Fred Armstrong said that the commissioners should hear about this, but nobody knew how to find them. Some other people said that Agnes brought it on herself, being so cheeky with Mr. Haskin and speaking up to the commissioners. But nobody defended Mr. Haskin.

I did not say anything because I'm just a girl and I don't know about these things. But I do know that Agnes was a kind and jolly person, who made our work fun whenever she could and was welcoming to a new doffer girl.

In the afternoon none of us worked very hard and it was very gloomy.

I took the paste-up of "The Day is Done" off Agnes's machine and put it in my pocket.

August 30

Dear Papa and Mama,

Such songs have power to quiet
The restless pulse of care,
And come like the benediction
That follows after prayer.

September 1

Dear Papa and Mama,

This is not a good week. I miss Agnes. Somebody said that she has gone to an older sister in Toronto. I hope she likes the big city. What I liked about Agnes was that she was not always obedient. In the Home I tried to be always obedient. This was not because I am such a good person, but because there was no choice. The disobedient ones just had a miserable time. But coming here to Almonte, living with Auntie and Uncle, I saw that they did not think very much about being obedient, and I started to think that when I was grown up I would not have to be so obedient. But now I think that there will always be a Mr. Haskin, someone to be obedient to.

I know that Auntie does not agree with me about Agnes, so I have nobody to tell, except Mungo.

September 3

Dear Papa and Mama,

One game that Mungo loves is to chase the end of a piece of wool. I drag the wool on the floor in front of him and he stares at it very intently and then he gives a great leap and grabs the end. Sometimes he slides along the floor and sometimes he flips right over, but he never gives up. Uncle says he is going to be a champion mouser.

Today when we got home from work and shopping we discovered that he had gotten into Auntie's knitting basket and pulled out a ball of wool and unwound it all over the kitchen. It was around chair legs and table legs and under the stove. One ball of wool is very long when Mungo gets hold of it. When we opened the door I felt scared for a second, thinking that Mungo and I would get into trouble. But Auntie and Uncle just laughed and Uncle called Mungo a scallywag and Auntie said it was like stepping into a spider's web. Thank goodness kittens get to be disobedient.

September 6

Dear Papa and Mama,

Today was a perfect warm day with a breeze, so Murdo and Kathleen and I gobbled our dinners and went for a fast ramble around town. We went past the high school and the students were on their break.

Some boys were playing baseball. The girls were sitting talking. I thought about Auntie and Uncle's plans for me to go to school. Perhaps I do want to. Truth: I don't know if I want to be a scholar, but I would like to sleep later in the morning and have nice schoolgirl clothes. I don't think these are proper reasons for going to high school. But nothing will change until next year so there's no point fretting about that.

September 10

Dear Papa and Mama,

Auntie and I have been in a flurry of cleaning. Uncle says that Auntie gets her spring cleaning urge in the fall. Every evening after work we've been hard at it. We've scrubbed and mopped and washed and dusted and polished and blacked the stove. Uncle has taken to going out. Mungo has taken to hiding under my bed.

September 11

Dear Papa and Mama,

Today was topsy-turvy. Murdo and Kathleen came up this afternoon and said that Mrs. Murphy had asked them to take some applesauce to Miss Steele and Miss Steele, and would I like to come. I didn't know at first who the Miss Steeles were, but then Murdo said, "You know. They wear dead squirrels around their necks." Kathleen boxed his ears for being disrespectful, but she was smiling nonetheless. And it did make me place who he meant.

Miss Steele and Miss Steele are two very old ladies at church. They are tall and thin as can be and their clothes are threadbare and sometimes not too clean. One has grey hair and one has white hair. But the most remarkable thing about them are these fur tippets that they wear, even in the summer. They are like a fur scarf with a tail on one end and a little head with beady glass eyes on the other. The mouth is a clip that bites the tail. The fur has worn thin, but the beady eyes are very bright and lifelike. Those animals and I have exchanged many stares during the Rev. Parfitt's sermons.

Auntie Janet said I could go. We walked out past the Cameronian Church and along the river. I kept looking for cottages but it just seemed to be countryside.

Then we came to a large stone house on a hill overlooking the river. I asked Kathleen if Miss Steele and Miss Steele were servants in the house and she said that it was their own house. I was flabbergasted. It was a grand house. They must be rich. Why did they look so poor?

Miss Steele and Miss Steele invited us in. They were wearing many layers of clothing (but no squirrels) and when we were shown into the parlour I understood why. It had the kind of cold of a place that has never been warm, and was very dim as well.

The room was full of furniture and so many things that I didn't know where to look first. Every inch of the walls was covered in paintings. Ships, forests, lovely ladies, dishes arranged on a table, storms at sea, vases of flowers. My eyes just went flit, flit, flit and didn't know where to stop, which is why I didn't really look at the chair before I sat in it, which is why I didn't see the chicken. You don't expect there to be a chicken in an armchair. The chicken did not like being sat upon and there was a great clucking and flying of feathers and I ended up on the floor. Kathleen just stood there with her mouth open and Murdo got the giggles, but Miss Steele and Miss Steele were not one bit bothered. They offered me a candy from a blackened silver dish. "Have a conversation lozenge," said grey-haired Miss Steele. "They are our favourites." Then she offered Murdo a cigar! "Father always enjoyed a cigar," said white-haired Miss Steele. Murdo looked as though he was going to take it when Kathleen jumped in and said that Murdo was too young to smoke. The chicken disappeared behind the settee and the conversation lozenges were passed once more and then Miss Steele and Miss Steele opened the paper bag with the jars of applesauce and they were delighted. Then grey-haired Miss Steele jumped up and removed a great number of pictures and ornaments and scarves from what turned out to be a piano and played us a piece of music. She played with gusto.

White-Steele burst into applause. "Charlotte is the musician. I am the artist. We might be twins but we have distinct gifts." She pointed to all the paintings on the walls. "All my own work."

"A gifted watercolourist," said Grey-Steele.

I knew that I could not look at Murdo. I knew that we would make each other laugh. Thank goodness for Kathleen, who made proper conversation, discussing grown-up things like the weather and the harvest.

We were just standing in the hall, on our way out, when the best/worst thing happened. There was a kind of knocking and scuffling noise and a large sheep wandered in from another room! "Oh, there you are, Polly," said Grey-Steele. "Polly is very fond of the vestibule."

That did it. Murdo had to pretend that he was having a coughing fit and he propelled himself out the front door. Kathleen and I managed to say goodbye properly, but once we were outside we had to run around the corner of the house before we burst with laughter.

On the walk home Kathleen told me what she knew of the story of the Steele family. Mr. Steele (the cigar-smoking father) had made a good deal of money with a grist mill and he built the big house. But then there was a dispute about water rights and he lost all his money and then he died and his two daughters, who never married, just went on living in the house.

"So are they poor?" I asked.

"Cash poor," said Kathleen. "Land rich."

Murdo just kept saying, "Polly is very fond of the vestibule."

Poor and rich at the same time. That's topsy-turvy.

September 12

Dear Papa and Mama,

Mr. Flanagan has announced that the mill is on half days this week. Something about wool supply being limited. I'll be happy to finish at noon each day, but Uncle James says it isn't such a happy story at payday.

September 13

Dear Papa and Mama,

One person who is completely happy about the half-day closing is Mungo. He thinks that the proper day for a human is the following:

Sleep in until 8:30.
From 8:30 to 9 give cat a good petting.
9 a.m. Get up and give cat cream.
9–12 Play "capture the wool" with cat.
12–3 Nap.
3–4 Pet cat.
4–5 Give cat more cream and a nice piece of fish.
5–8 Play "jump into a paper sack" with cat.

8–9 Provide snack for cat (liver is good), pet cat.
9 p.m. Cat goes outside to his own secret life.

September 14

Dear Papa and Mama,

We have much more time this week for reading the newspaper. The story by Mr. Wilkie Collins about the Countess Narona is getting scarier and scarier. Everyone is thinking that the Countess murdered Lord Montbarry for his money. I'm sure the story is already unsuitable for me, but we all long to know what is going to happen so we are not talking about suitable or unsuitable.

September 16

Dear Papa and Mama,

Uncle James has been going fishing every afternoon this week. I am not extremely fond of fish, but Mungo is happy.

September 17

Dear Papa and Mama,

Uncle James was right. It was a thin payday today. There will be no cream for Mungo this week. But Auntie said that we should pretend it had been a holiday week, just like Lord Montbarry and the Countess have, but instead of going to Venice we should go to the concert at the town hall. The concert was given by the students from the high school.

The hall was full to bursting. There were recitations and music, but the very best thing was the "Broom Brigade." Nine girls, a few years older than me, were dressed a bit like soldiers, but instead of rifles and bayonets they had brooms and dustpans. Their teacher, Mr. Tullis, called out commands like "Prepare for cavalry!" and then they all moved together, in a drill, holding out their brooms or snapping to attention, brooms at their shoulders. It was very pleasing, the patterns they made, a bit like the patterns of weaving. They finished by sweeping their way out. The audience liked it so much that they clapped and clapped until the girls had to do the whole thing again.

On the way home Uncle James called me Captain Rutherford and we all did a bit of marching, but Auntie and I agreed that real sweeping isn't this much fun. Then we talked about what would it be like if all the women got together and swept and cleaned through everybody's house in smart military formation. Auntie Janet said that once they were finished with everybody's house she would call out, "At ease!" and all the women would sit down and have tea and laugh and tell stories.

September 18

Dear Papa and Mama,

It has been quite the week for armies. This evening Murdo and Kathleen and I were just coming back from the river, where Murdo and I had been practising rock skipping, when we heard the sounds of a band from the direction of Mr. Mitcheson's store. When we got there we saw that the Citizen's Band were giving a concert under the electric light. But just as they finished one piece we heard the same piece being played in the distance and then we saw, marching down the street, the Salvation Army with *their* band. So then the leader of the Citizen's Band got the band to join in again and soon everybody was playing the same song. The Salvation Army marched by and everybody kept playing. By the time the Salvation Army got back to the electric light on their return trip a huge crowd had gathered between the Almonte House and the No. 2 weave room. Even Mr. Flanagan and his wife and son were there. And everybody was singing and clapping along. The only bad thing was that at the end some mean boys from the high school started to throw eggs at the Salvation Army. Why do boys have to be this way? If I had a brother perhaps I would understand.

September 22

Dear Papa and Mama,

The world of Mr. Wilkie Collins is not the only place where there are mysteries and criminals. There is one right here in Almonte. On the way to the mill this morning I noticed a poster on the big tree at the edge of the Agricultural Grounds. I read it out to Auntie and Uncle. It read, *STOP HORSE THIEF,* and it went on to describe a dark brown horse with a white spot on his nose and white hind feet that had been stolen from a Mr. Dick Langford.

"Oh, I know that horse," said Uncle James. "It is driven by that skinny, sour-looking old man who comes in on market day." The poster went on to describe the thief as George Goodwin, alias St. George, alias Brennan, height such and such, weight so and so, sandy colouring, age twenty-four, sharp features and so on. The poster said that if anybody saw the man he was to "take charge of any horse he has" and wire the County Constable.

I didn't know the word *alias,* but I figured out that it must mean someone using many names. I didn't know you were allowed to call yourself after a saint.

Uncle James said it was a pity that the poster did not mention a reward. Otherwise we could all go horse-thief hunting and become rich.

September 23

Dear Papa and Mama,

Today we had another half-day holiday. Uncle James says we must be careful not to get used to this or we'll be wanting to live a life of leisure, like mill owners.

The reason for the holiday is the Fall Exhibition. We walked to the Agricultural Grounds right after noon and we were in time to see the driving contests. There were contests for best lady rider on horseback, best gentleman rider on horseback, ladies' driving (single horse) and ladies' driving (team), and the same for gentlemen and for boys under sixteen. The horses were all decked out and so were the people. It wasn't as wonderful as Charles Fish at the circus, though. Then there was a one-mile bicycle race. Murdo says that if he had three magic wishes he would use one on having a bicycle, and even if he had only one magic wish he would still use it on having a bicycle.

Inside the Exhibition Hall there were more tables with all kinds of fruit and vegetables, including a pumpkin so big I couldn't reach my arms around it. The winning entries had ribbons on them. There were flowers and preserves and all kinds of handiwork. There were rag rugs and shawls and stockings and mitts and patchwork. Auntie and I spent a long time looking at the knitting and crochet, embroidery and tatting. We decided that next year we will start very early and have something to enter. There was a contest for "fancy pincushion by a girl under fourteen years" won by somebody called Minnie Prentice. It wasn't that good. I think I could do very well at a fancy pincushion next year.

The exhibits of baking (pies, bread, cakes, cookies, tarts) made us all very hungry so we treated ourselves to tea with cakes at the refreshment tent.

Then we went out again to look at the animals (horses, cows, pigs, chickens). My favourites were the heavy draft horses. They look so strong and patient.

September 24

Dear Papa and Mama,

Tonight was sheep-shearing night. This is what Uncle James calls it when Auntie cuts our hair. She takes great care and trouble with us, making sure that everything comes out even. When she cuts Uncle's hair she moans about cowlicks, but she's only pretending. With me she brushes and brushes and then cuts one comb-full at a time. I closed my eyes and it was as though it was you, Mama. The lovely sound of the scissors, the feeling of having my face touched and turned one way and the other for a final inspection. I wanted it to go on for much longer than it did.

September 27

Dear Papa and Mama,

When we were on our dinner hour today, Murdo's father came up to the spinning room to tell us news of a murder. He told us that Mr. Langford, the old man whose horse was stolen, had been found murdered in his barn. A few days ago Mr. Langford's neighbour noticed that the old man wasn't out working, so he went across to check up on him and found his body in the barn. Someone had hit him on the head with an iron bar. The police have called in a detective to try to find out who did it. Of course we all wondered if it was the man on the poster. But we did not feel like joking about him now.

September 29

Dear Papa and Mama,

More talk of the murder today. Murdo's father knows the cousin of the County Constable, who told him that the detective made a very surprising and odd discovery. It seems that there were muddy footprints in Mr. Langford's house and on his bed that were not the footprints of Mr. Langford himself. The footprints were those of a thick wet stained sock. "It looks like the murderer did the old man in and then went to sleep in his bed." And there's more.

It turns out that the horse-thief man was known to wear leather moccasins. "Sounds like a pretty good match for a thick wet sock to me," said Murdo's father.

I'm glad and not glad that Mr. Campbell came to tell us this story. As a made-up story it is good, with the detective and the mystery and all. But when I think of an old man lying dying in his barn all night while the murderer sleeps in his cozy bed, it makes me sad and frightened. And it's not in some faraway city or distant land, but right here. I hope they find the murderer and lock him up.

September 30

Dear Papa and Mama,

There was another part of the Lord Montbarry story in the newspaper today, but we did not feel like reading about murders, even in a story.

October 1

Dear Papa and Mama,

October. I do not like the word *October.* October is the saddest month. Of course I am thinking especially of you. When I first arrived at the Home there was one kind person there, Cook. She was the only person who ever talked about you. She found me crying one day and she hugged me and said, "October is a terrible month for dying." I didn't know what she meant. I was only five — nearly six. I still don't know what she meant. Is any month a good month for dying? But she made me feel less lonely. She smelled like apples. Or maybe it was you, Mama, who smelled like apples.

Cucumber 2

Dear Papa and Mama,

After church today Kathleen and Murdo and I went to sit by the falls. Even though it was warm and pleasant I was not cheerful. Kathleen, who is a kind person when she is not being superior, noticed the cloud I was under, and I ended up telling them about why I do not like October. At first they did not know what to say, but then Murdo picked up a large hunk of wood and chucked it into the river. "That's October," he said, "gone. Now we just need to find another name for the time between September and November."

We decided it should be a word ending in the sound "ber" and we tried *timber* and *remember* and *number* and then Murdo thought of *cucumber*, which made us all laugh. So Cucumber it is.

Today there was a missionary in church, from Asia Minor. He had a wonderful fancy name: Garabed Nergarian. He wore a beautiful oriental costume and sang a hymn in Armenian. I'm sure it is the strangest hymn ever sung in St. John's Church. I wonder how you get to be a missionary? Probably you need to be very clever, to learn other languages and such.

Cucumber 3

Dear Papa and Mama,

Sometimes at the mill the noise of the machines makes the same words go around and around in my head. Today the words were *Garabed Nergarian.* I take Agnes's poem with me every day in my pocket, but I don't read it because it makes me sad to think of her, but now I think it is time to learn another verse so that I have something new to say to myself.

Cucumber 4

Dear Papa and Mama,

I have a new verse by heart now:

Then read from the treasured volume
The poem of thy choice,
And lend to the rhyme of the poet
The beauty of thy voice.

Cucumber 6

Dear Papa and Mama,

Dreadful time lighting the stove this morning. When I'm up before Auntie and Uncle I light the stove and make the tea. But this morning was a disaster. I cleaned out the ashes and laid the fire with paper and kindling as usual. But then the smoke just started coming into the room. And I didn't know what to do. I did not want to douse it with water for that would make a horrible mess.

Just when I thought I would have to go for help, Uncle James came into the room. He put the fire out and then he showed me how to light a bit of paper and hold it up the stovepipe for a minute or two before lighting the fire. "Days like this," he said, "damp and still, the chimney won't draw unless the air is warmed first." I said I was sorry, but he did not chide me at all. He opened the window and aired out the room. When Auntie Janet got up she said that we both smelled smoky. "Yes," he said, "that Mr. Haskin will be wanting to fry up Flora for breakfast, like bacon. I'd let him if I were you. He needs a bit of fattening up, that one."

Cucumber 8

Dear Papa and Mama,

The weather is getting cooler. Time for new shoes

— mine have been good shoes, but they are getting small. At the Home our shoes came in the charity bales and mostly they did not fit well, but this last time I was lucky and my shoes were just the right size, with plenty of wear left in them, but now they pinch. I wish I could persuade my feet to stop growing. The shoes are fine for the short walk to church, but I do not think I will manage the walk to the mill. I don't want to ask Auntie and Uncle for new shoes, as they are very expensive.

Cucumber 9

Dear Papa and Mama,

Mrs. Parfitt, the minister's wife, has started a Bible Study class in the afternoon after church, at the rectory. Auntie Janet and I decided to go. There are about ten in the class. Auntie and I and Maggie Menzies are the only ones from the mill. Mrs. Parfitt served tea in pretty teacups and there were scones.

After the Bible Study and the scones Mrs. Parfitt read us a poem. It was written by a mill girl many years ago. I didn't know that ordinary people could be poets. It began, "We, who must toil and spin, What clothing shall we wear?" and it was all about God weaving and spinning, through the rain and sun of heaven. "Wherethrough for us his spindles run, His mighty shuttles fly." At the end God weaves "finest webs of light" for all who toil and spin.

I loved the way the poet used ordinary words like *spindles* and *shuttles* alongside fancy words like *vesture* and *raiment* instead of just plain old *clothes.* It made me think of you, in heaven, wearing white vestures and raiments and having sun and rain and space of sky. I never before thought of rain in heaven.

Cucumber 10

Dear Papa and Mama,

Today Auntie said that the question in the mill girl's poem, "We, who must toil and spin, What clothing shall we wear?" reminded her that I need some warmer clothes and shoes for winter and that next Saturday we will buy some fabric. I remembered my socks for Uncle James. I am going to start on them again. Auntie is knitting a shawl.

Cucumber 11

Dear Papa and Mama,

Big news of yesterday was a fire. But it was an on-purpose one. The firemen wanted to practise using their new fire boat so they gathered a big pile of brush on the riverbank by the town hall. Murdo and I went down to see. It was a huge blaze and hundreds of people gathered. In the light of the fire everyone, even the people I know — faces from the mill, and from the shops and church, even Murdo — looked like strangers. Not *exactly* like strangers. I could recognize Rev. Parfitt or Mr. Cunningham from the grocery store, but it was like they were themselves, but fairies. The fairy butcher. The fairy teacher. I suppose I looked like the fairy Flora.

When the blaze became very huge the firemen sprayed out water from giant hoses. There were great cheers from the crowd. Murdo said that he wants to be a fireman.

Cucumber 15

Dear Papa and Mama,

Today was shopping day. After work Auntie and I went to the dry goods store. We bought stuff for two dresses, one for her and one for me, and some flannel for a shirt for Uncle. My dress is to be blue with small white flowers, Auntie's brown. The shirt will be grey. I bought a ball of crochet cotton with my pay, as Auntie says that she is going to teach me to crochet lace. We took a long time over the shopping and looked at everything. I thought we were finished when Auntie surprised me by saying that she had noticed that I needed new shoes.

I am now the proud owner of my first pair of brand new shoes. They are lovely, shiny dark brown, like a horse. My toes have room to wiggle with joy and they do. I did not wear them home because I want to save them.

When we got home we decided to cut out our dresses right away while the light was still good. Uncle grumbled about where was supper and he was not that interested in the flannel for his shirt. He is not interested in vesture and raiment at all. We teased him that there was cold porridge for supper and then we thought, "What a good idea." So we all had cold porridge and then we had applesauce and it was very good too.

I have put my shoes beside my bed so that I can look at them first thing in the morning. Mungo keeps trying to crawl into them.

Cucumber 16

Dear Papa and Mama,

No Bible Study today because Mrs. Parfitt is away, visiting her ill mother in Arnprior.

Auntie and I spent half the afternoon finishing cutting out our dresses and the other half with me learning to crochet. I have a plan to crochet a band of lace to put around the neck of my new dress. Mungo was a dreadful nuisance with the crocheting. Finally Uncle picked him up and carried him around on his shoulder. Mungo's favourite place, after my bed, is next to Uncle's face.

Cucumber 17

Dear Papa and Mama,

I wore my shoes to work today. I tried to walk very carefully so as not to crack the tops of them. Murdo asked me why I was walking like a chicken. As soon as I got to the mill I took them off to save them.

Cucumber 19

Dear Papa and Mama,

Auntie and I have been sewing every night and now our dresses are almost finished. Just in time for me because today I did a long reach for a broken thread and the sleeve ripped right out of my dress at the shoulder. I mended it this evening, but truly the dress is too small.

Cucumber 20

Dear Papa and Mama,

Today was Harvest Festival at church. The church was beautifully decorated with flowers and vegetables and we sang, "Come ye thankful people come, raise the song of harvest-home; All is safely gathered in, ere the winter storms begin." I looked down at my new dress, which has some gathering on the sleeves, and I felt safely gathered in even though I know that is not what it means.

Cucumber 21

Dear Papa and Mama,

Everyone in the spinning room said nice things about my new dress. It didn't take but an hour, of course, before it was all covered with tufts of wool.

Cucumber 23

Dear Papa and Mama,

Church and Bible Study today. Scones again, but no more poetry.

Cucumber 24

Dear Papa and Mama,

Murdo Campbell is a most vexing person. Yesterday I was thinking he was one of the kindest people I've ever met and today he was such a know-it-all. Today he was talking about telephones. I know about telephones. There are telephones in Almonte. There is one at the mill. I've seen one at the livery stable. Murdo needn't think that he knows more than I do about everything. But today he took it upon himself to explain to me how they work. He said that sound carries down the wire like water goes through a pipe. This cannot be true. Water is a real thing and pipes are hollow. Sound is, well, sound and wires aren't hollow. So then he asked me how I thought telephones worked and I didn't really have an answer. I did think of answering "magic," but Murdo just rolls his eyes when I talk about magic. Then he said he would prove to me how telephones worked because he was going to build one. I said the day he built a telephone was the day that I would fly and he said, "Done!" as though it were a bargain. Sound down pipes — silliness.

Moon-Shadow and Sundew and Bladderwort don't need telephones. Their whispers are carried on the wind.

Cucumber 25

Dear Papa and Mama,

Oh, how the mighty are fallen. Not that I'm the mighty, but I am surely fallen. Murdo is right again. He came over after supper with a contraption made of two tin cans joined with a long length of string. We went outside and I held one tin up to my ear and he walked away the distance of the string, keeping it tight between us. Then he talked into the other tin and, sure enough, I could hear him clearly, even though he was talking normally. "Hello, Miss Rutherford," he said. "When can we expect to see you fly?" Then he laughed and I could have heard that even without the telephone. I'm still sure there must be more to telephones than that, but I wasn't in a position to argue. Also, although I wasn't going to let Murdo know, I was quite impressed by the contrivance. I wonder if we could run it inside, from his room to mine.

So now I guess I have to fly, which means I hope that hot-air balloonist comes back to Almonte.

Cucumber 29

Dear Papa and Mama,

This morning I woke up even before the train whistle so I took a notion to go outside and watch the train go by. It is grand to be up earlier than everyone, alone in the world like Adam and Eve maybe (but with clothes; I was all wrapped up in my shawl). I was careful not to wash my face in dew because I did not want to be stolen away by a wizard. (Well, there wasn't any dew, only frost, but I was careful anyway.) I was not alone long, though, because soon a man came running by, down John Street. He was wearing short pants and a singlet even though the weather is quite cold. He didn't appear to be chasing something, nor was anything chasing him. He smiled as he ran by.

Then I went in and lit the stove.

Later I told Uncle James and he said that the runner was named John Sullivan and he is a weaver at the mill. He runs to Appleton and back before he comes to work in the morning. That is ten miles! I asked Uncle James why and he said just for the joy of it. John Sullivan must certainly be one of those early-morning people, akin to chickens.

Cucumber 30

Dear Papa and Mama,

This morning Rev. Parfitt talked about saints because All Saints' Day is coming up on Tuesday. He said that the church makes saints of people who do extraordinary, miraculous things, but that it was also a day to think about all the people who came before us, who made it possible for us to be here today. Auntie reached over and took my hand because she knew that I was thinking about you both.

We walked home with Murdo and Kathleen. Uncle James said he hoped we noticed that he was the only one of us with a proper saint's name. Murdo said that there was a Saint Murdo, but nobody had heard of him because he was an Armenian saint from Asia Minor. None of us believes that for a minute.

Cucumber 31

Dear Papa and Mama,

Dinnertime. Today is Hallowe'en. We didn't have Hallowe'en at the Home, but now I'm finding out about it. Mrs. Murphy, who is Irish, says that they leave out a bowl of milk for the fairies because tonight is the night they roam abroad. Murdo says that it is the night for boys to play tricks. I asked Kathleen what girls do and she said that it is a good night to foretell the future. She says she'll come over tonight and show me how. Auntie and Uncle don't know much about Hallowe'en except that Auntie says it would be a good night for a story of witches, and a good night to keep Mungo inside because sometimes the boys' tricks are cruel to cats.

November 1

Dear Papa and Mama,

This morning as we walked to work we noticed everybody on Mill Street pointing and laughing. Some Hallowe'en roustabouts had put new signs on many of the businesses. Here is what they said:

On the doctor's office: *Undertaker and Practical Embalmer*
On the tavern: *Bible Depository*
On the milliner's: *Hats for Horses*
On the barber's: *Tonsorial Artist*
On the livery stable: *French Perfumes*

Everybody was saying it was the work of the high-school boys. Uncle James said, "Only the moon knows and she's not telling."

By the time work was over everything was put to rights. This was one day when I was glad to be up and in town before seven o'clock to see it all.

While all the businesses were being renamed, Kathleen and I were telling the future. She came upstairs after supper and she showed me how to predict the man you'll marry. You peel an apple and throw the apple peeling over your left shoulder and when it falls it makes the shape of the first letter of the name of the man you will marry. Hers was C. Mine was either a U or a J or a flipped-over L. Uncle James said that he feels sorry for all the Arthurs and Alfreds and Andrews, for when would an apple peel fall in the shape of an A? Then Auntie told ghost stories. I went outside last thing to have a look for fairies, but no luck.

November 5

Dear Papa and Mama,

Snow this morning. And cold. It is suddenly winter. I was very glad of my new shoes and my shawl. Mungo went out the window this morning and as soon as his paws touched the snow he pulled them up in horror and gave me a look that said, "Do something about this right now!"

The warmth of the mill was welcome.

November 6

Dear Papa and Mama,

I went to Bible Study without Auntie Janet today. She had something to do at home, but she would not say what. At Bible Study we talked about when David is angry and he's going to kill Nabal and Nabal's wife Abigail smoothes everything over and tells David that his life is carried by the Lord in a bundle. Mrs. Parfitt told us that in Bible times people did not have satchels or trunks, so they put their most precious things in a bundle when they had to move them from one place to another.

Mrs. Parfitt served tiny tea pancakes with jam. It took me an effort to only eat a polite number. I've changed my mind about what manna is.

November 7

Dear Papa and Mama,

More snow. There is ice at the edge of the river. Mungo has changed his mind and now he loves bouncing around in the snow.

November 10

Dear Papa and Mama,

There was a surprise visitor in the spinning room this morning. I had just finished doffing the frame when I saw someone, out of the corner of my eye, walking in the alley between the frames. I got the impression of someone large and angry. I turned to look and I saw a rough-looking man with a scraggly beard and a pack on his back. He stopped at the frame of Mrs. Brown and I saw her turn. She gave a little cry and then she turned white, like a piece of paper. The man started to yell and wave his fist in the air and Mrs. Brown was trying to edge away from him. Then Mr. Haskin appeared and he went up to the man, but the man just grabbed him by the coat and tossed him away, like you would toss away an apple core.

Auntie Janet grabbed my arm and said, "Get James, quick." I practically flew down the stairs. All I could say to Uncle James was "Come quick" and he came running. Some of the other men set off after him. I could not climb the stairs as fast as they did, so by the time I got up Uncle James had the rough man pinned against the wall. Mrs. Brown was sitting on the floor and some of the women were fanning her. Mrs. Campbell was holding a hankie against Mr. Haskin's bleeding nose. Soon thereafter Mr. Flanagan came with a policeman and he took the rough man away. Mr. Flanagan said that Mrs. Brown should take the rest of the day off, but she said a cup of tea was all she needed. Mr. Haskin went home to change his bloody shirt.

Now it is dinnertime and Auntie Janet is sitting

with Mrs. Brown. They are having a long talk. I went to join them, but Auntie looked up at me and shook her head. So I'm writing this instead.

November 11

Dear Papa and Mama,

This evening Auntie told me about Mrs. Brown. The rough man is her husband. We thought that Mrs. Brown was a widow, but that is just a story that she told when she came to Almonte to look for work. She ran away from her husband, taking her children with her, because he was a drinking man and violent with it. She said that she was afraid for herself and the children. She thought she was safe in Almonte but now he has found her again and he won't let her alone.

I thought about Miss Beulah Young and the temperance pledge. Suddenly the stories she told seemed very real. I don't think I'm going to get married. Or, if I do, I am going to make sure that my husband has signed the pledge.

November 13

Dear Papa and Mama,

After church today we went to see Mrs. Brown. I took the Brown children for a walk while the adults visited. Down by the river I met up with Murdo, who tagged along. The two little girls are dear, but five-year-old Charlie is a horror, given to kicking. I guess I know why now, with such a father. He kept trying to run out onto the ice on the river and I had to keep chasing him because the ice isn't safe yet.

The only thing that made him happy on the walk was when Murdo fought with him. Charlie kept punching and Murdo, who is very strong, just kept him at arm's length, but didn't mock him. I could see that Charlie wasn't really wanting to hit Murdo, but just hit out at anything. Then Charlie got tired and Murdo told him that he could become a prize-fighter and then Murdo gave him a piggyback ride home.

November 16

Dear Papa and Mama,

Today I am twelve years old and the happiest girl in Almonte, or maybe all of Ontario. I did not mention my birthday to Auntie Janet and Uncle James. I do remember a birthday with you. I remember a skipping rope and a doll with a blue dress named Wee One (what happened to Wee One?), but at the Home we did not celebrate birthdays because Matron said that if we did it for one we would have to do it for all. That was often the way there — there were many things we could not do because it would not be fair. But in a family I guess you can do things for everybody. But back to my story of the day.

When I got up this morning there was a large brown paper parcel on the table. Auntie and Uncle were just waiting for me to wake up. I opened it before I even washed. It was a dress. It is beautiful, a dress for a princess. Auntie cut down a dress of her own that was worn and she is so clever that she made a dress that looks like new. It is made of wool in a colour so deep red that it just makes you warm to look at it. Now I know what she was doing on Sundays afternoons when she wasn't at Bible Study.

I could not even talk. I tried to say thank you, but I just burst out crying. Uncle James was worried and thought that something was wrong, but Auntie understood. She told me that she thought it was time I had a Sunday dress now that I'm growing up and that I could sew some of my crocheted lace onto the collar.

Then Uncle said that Mungo had a present for me too and he reached into the woodbox where Mungo likes to hide in the morning, and pulled him out and he had two shiny blue hair ribbons around his neck!

I wondered how I could bear to wait for Sunday to wear my new dress. I think being twelve is grand.

November 17

Dear Papa and Mama,

Today it is Thanksgiving, but we do not have a holiday because it is a busy time at the mill. Mr. Flanagan has many orders to fill. Between bobbins I thought about thankfulness, though. I am truly thankful, for Auntie and Uncle, for Mungo, and for my new red dress.

November 18

Dear Papa and Mama,

I read in the *Gazette* today that the Canada Atlantic Railway has equipped their trains with electric lights. Electric light would be a very welcome thing in that black tunnel out of Brockville.

November 20

Dear Papa and Mama,

Sunday, and a chance to wear my new dress. Soon I will change out of it to save it, but I just want to wear it for part of the afternoon. I feel like a new person in it.

November 23

Dear Papa and Mama,

Mr. Flanagan is constructing something on his property, between the Point and the railway track.

There are posts in the ground, high at one end, low at the other. It does not look like a building, but it is going to be big.

November 24

Dear Papa and Mama,

Of course Murdo knows what Mr. Flanagan is building. I would be peeved that Murdo is a know-it-all yet again, except that I have no time for peeving because the news is so exciting. It is to be a toboggan run!

November 26

Dear Papa and Mama,

The toboggan run is finished. It officially opened today and we all went to look at it. Mr. Flanagan lets the mill workers use it for free in the evenings. It looks like the most glorious fun, but of course we do not have a toboggan.

Murdo did not let that stop him. He ran home and came back with an iron scoop shovel. He went down the slide spinning around and when he got to the bottom he jumped up lickety-split and sat himself right down in the snow. I guess the shovel heated up some, sliding on that icy slope. The boys were shouting, "In the hot seat, Murd?" But then he just went and did it again.

I long to do it, and lots of girls and even women were whooshing down, but I would have to do it on a shovel and I know that would not be proper.

November 27

Dear Papa and Mama,

In church today Rev. Parfitt said that the text for his sermon was going to be about tobogganing. Psalm 26, Verse 1: "I have trusted also in the Lord; therefore I shall not slide." At first I thought he was serious and that he would say that tobogganing was sinful, but he was joking. I saw Mrs. Parfitt shaking her head. I don't think she approves of jokes in a sermon.

November 29

Dear Papa and Mama,

There is so much to tell you about this evening. As we were walking home we saw Mr. McFarlane, from the dry goods store, and little Millie McFarlane travelling along in their cutter. The moon was bright. It was being pulled by their lovely brown and white horse. He's called Billy. They were stopped at the railway crossing near the bridge. But when the train sounded its whistle the horse panicked and jumped ahead, pulling the cutter across the tracks.

Mr. McFarlane yelled and then he picked up

Millie and threw her into a snowbank and then he whipped the reins and tried to get Billy to move, but he wouldn't. So then Mr. McFarlane jumped out of the cutter himself. The shunting engine came across the bridge with brakes squealing. It hit the cutter and smashed it to bits. Then Billy panicked even more and ran down the steep bank, onto the ice on the river, dragging all the wrecked cutter behind him.

Then, there was just noise and darkness and confusion and Billy disappeared. Suddenly one of the men shouted, "There he is!"

I looked down. It was even darker on the river, but I thought I saw Billy standing on the ice. But then there was a great crack and that terrible sound of a horse screaming and somebody shouted, "He's gone under." Mr. McFarlane rushed by me and put little Millie into my arms. Then he and Uncle James and some of the other mill men slithered down to the shore.

There was shouting. I could not see what was happening, but soon we saw them leading Billy onto firm ground. Little Millie was just snugged into me. I just kept telling her that she was safe and Billy was safe and everybody was safe. Then Mr. McFarlane came and collected her, and Auntie Janet and I went home. Uncle James stayed to help with Billy. This all happened in less time than it takes to write it down.

Time is not always like an ever-rolling stream, but like a rushing river.

November 30

Dear Papa and Mama,

Great surprise today. Mr. McFarlane came by the house today, after supper. He said that Billy is fine and then he told Uncle James that he had never seen a man with a better way of calming a horse. "I would have lost him if it had not been for you." And then he thanked me for taking care of Millie.

He brought us two thank-you presents. The small present was a bag of candies, Scotch mixture. A mint is in my mouth right now. I'm making it last as long as possible. The big present is the splendid thing. It is a toboggan! We none of us ever thought we would have a toboggan. Mr. McFarlane says that he had it from when he was a boy, but that Mrs. McFarlane doesn't care for tobogganing and that Millie is too small. We cannot wait to try it. Is a toboggan as fast as a train? It looks even faster. What is the fastest thing in the world?

December 1

Dear Papa and Mama,

Today was the longest day ever at the mill, or maybe in the history of the world. This morning as we walked by the slide I imagined going down it and all day long I heard the machine say "To-bogg-an-ing, to-bogg-an-ing."

But now I can tell you that tobogganing is the most glorious thing, as good as imagining! The first time we all went together. Auntie Janet was on the front, then me (the filling in the sandwich), then Uncle James on the back. The moment before you push off it is as though the whole world goes still. Then off you go, a little sticky at first, and then you're off, faster than fast. I buried my head in Auntie's back and held on to her for dear life. I couldn't see anything (my eyes were closed, to tell the truth), but there was a lovely swishing sound. At the bottom there was a bit of a bump and the toboggan went right up in the air and that's when Uncle James started whooping. Then I went just with Uncle James so I got to see, which was even scarier and more splendid. Then I went by myself and nearly steered right off the track and ended up tipping over and everyone laughed and whooped, but in a friendly way.

Once in the lineup there were some schoolgirls standing behind me and one of them said, "Oh, this must be the free time for the mill workers." I don't care. Her fancy clothes did not make her go faster and she was not courageous enough to ride on her own. She did a lot of squealing. I whoop, but I do not squeal.

On one run Auntie and Uncle fell off and they rolled over and over in the snow all cuddled up together and laughing and laughing and they didn't get up right away and I heard Mrs. Ramsay (bouncing feather hat) from church say, "Well, I never," in a disapproving way and I wanted to say, "What do you never? Do you never cuddle with Mr. Ramsay?"

When I was waiting in the line I asked Auntie what she thought would happen if we all said out loud what we think inside our heads and she laughed and said that there would be rioting in the streets.

Murdo came by right at the end and he told me that toboggans can reach speeds of ninety miles an hour. So that answers the question of what is the fastest thing in the world. Of course we let him join in.

We tobogganed until dark, until we were more than half frozen and we could hardly climb another step. I'm putting tobogganing in a bundle in my mind to remember for always.

December 2

Dear Papa and Mama,

There was a poem in the newspaper today about tobogganing.

The rollum has vanished
The skatum has fled
The rinkum is banished
The wheelum is dead
Tobog's now the daisy
That now rules the day
Let's tobog till we're crazy
O lally dum day.

Uncle said it wasn't quite true because the rinkum isn't banished. In fact, there is going to be a curling bonspiel at the rink next week. But we all agreed that tobog is certainly the daisy.

December 3

Dear Papa and Mama,

Auntie and I did the shopping in a great hurry after work this afternoon so that we could tobog till we were crazy. All the Campbells came. Murdo wanted to try to fit the whole family on the toboggan together, but Mrs. Campbell wouldn't let them take the little ones. But they got Kathleen, Murdo, Percy and Archie all squeezed on like sardines in a can. Some of the bigger boys try to go down standing up on the toboggan, but nobody has succeeded yet.

We came home crazy, wet and exhausted.

Mungo has a new pleasure. He likes you to drip

water on his head. He purrs and rolls around and tries to bat the drips with his paw. I thought cats were supposed to hate water.

December 4

Dear Papa and Mama,

Morning. I hear Uncle lighting the stove, but I'm going to stay in bed until it is warmer. I hear that slide calling, "Flora Rutherford, come and slide on me." But of course it is Sunday. I wish it weren't. Is that wicked?

Evening. It was a sunny, sparkly day, and even though Mrs. Parfitt served delicious gingerbread at Bible Study I still heard the voice of that empty toboggan slide.

Instead of sliding, we knitted. My socks are nearly done. Auntie says I can give them to Uncle as a Christmas present. I have not had occasion to give presents before. What can I get Auntie? This is a very pleasant question to think about. I have one dollar saved.

December 5

Dear Papa and Mama,

Murdo told me that every year there is a big Christmas party for all the mill workers at the town hall, not just for the workers at the woollen mill, but from the knitting mill too. He said that there is a huge decorated tree and mince tarts and cherry cake and ginger beer and presents. "And dancing, but I don't like that part." He said that Mr. Flanagan pays for it all. We had a Christmas party at the Home too, but not with adults and we didn't have dancing.

December 8

Dear Papa and Mama,

Today there was a letter from Uncle James's brother, Wilfred Duncan. He lives way out west in British Columbia on a ranch. He has a big family. "He's not much of a one for writing," said Auntie Janet, "but we do get the news every year come Christmas." Then, "I must write back and tell him our big news of the year." It took me a minute to realize that she meant me. Flora Rutherford — big news. She asked if I would help with the letter, so that is what we did this evening.

December 9

Dear Papa and Mama,

There was another tobogganing poem in the paper today. Auntie Janet says that the trick of hiding the word *tobogganing* in it is like weaving. Here it is:

The winter sports include a new
But **O**mnipresent pleasure;
And lively **B**oys, and maidens, too,
Happy mem**O**ries treasure
Of first tobo**G**anning delights
When down the **G**lassy shutelets
They flashed like sw**A**llows in their flights,
And showed their fa**N**cy bootlets.
Long may this winter fu**N** remain,
To please the country's mill**I**ons
And each January come agai**N**
Until we've **G**rown to billions.

I've never heard the word *shutelet,* but maybe in poems you're allowed to make up the words you need or put in an extra "n" so that winter's fun can remain.

Tomorrow I'm going to have a look around the general store and see what Christmas presents can be had for a dollar. Perhaps I could give Murdo a present too.

December 15

Dear Papa and Mama,

I have not written in days because something terrible has happened. Uncle James has been hurt at the mill. It happened on Monday. The first we knew was when Mr. Haskin came into the spinning room at a run and said that Auntie Janet and I must come right away. We went down to the weave room and there was Uncle James on the floor, covered in blood. His eyes were closed and he wasn't moving. I thought he was dead. Auntie Janet screamed and threw herself down upon him. Dr. Reeve appeared with some bandages and water and he started to wipe away some of the blood. Then Uncle James woke up and started saying that he was fine, he was fine, but of course he was not fine at all. The blood was coming from his right arm and hand which looked like

I cannot finish that sentence. It did not look like an arm at all, but more like meat.

Dr. Reeve bandaged the arm and then they put Uncle James on a board and carried him home. When Dr. Reeve came he gave Uncle James a drink of brandy and then he bound his arm to a wooden splint and sewed up the cuts in his arm and hand. I could not look. Uncle James did not cry or complain once, but instead tried to talk to the doctor.

The doctor gave Uncle James some pills for the pain.

For the past three days we have just sat with Uncle James. Mrs. Campbell and Granny Whitall have been bringing us soup and tea, but Auntie Janet does not eat anything. She is very busy all the time, taking care of Uncle James, but when she stops for a minute she just stares.

I am trying to be helpful and good, but I do not really know what to do.

Mr. Boothroyd came by this evening and asked what happened. Uncle James does not remember how it happened, but he got his arm caught between the belt and a pulley. He keeps saying how foolish he was and blaming himself.

When I ask Auntie Janet if Uncle James will be all right she just says that we must pray as hard as we can for him to be well.

When I close my eyes I just keep seeing the same picture over and over again. It is a picture of Auntie Janet stained with blood and her hair all hanging down when she stood up to let Mr. Reeve bandage Uncle James. Auntie Janet is usually so clean and tidy. I cannot write any more.

December 16

Dear Papa and Mama,

Rev. Parfitt came to visit today. He brought a pan of buns from Mrs. Parfitt.

We were sitting at the table when Mungo jumped up on my knee and then, quick as a wink, onto the table. He was heading toward the cream jug. Uncle made as if to rescue the cream and then he made the most terrible yelp and he turned white as paper and sweat broke out on his face. Auntie tried to get him to take one of the pills, but he just banged on the table with his other hand and said no.

December 17

Dear Papa and Mama,

Uncle James is worse. His arm and his hand turned a horrible dark colour and then he started to run a fever. Dr. Reeve came again and he talked to Auntie Janet and then they sent me away, to stay with Granny Whitall for the night. Granny Whitall was very kind and made scones for me. But they were just sawdust in my mouth. And then because Granny Whitall was kind it made me very soft and wobbly. I cried and cried.

That was last night and this morning I came home again and Auntie Janet told me that Dr. Reeve had to cut off three of Uncle James's fingers.

The good news now is that the fever has gone down and Uncle James drank a bit of soup. The good news is so little and the bad news is so big.

December 18

Dear Papa and Mama,

Why are sick people so frightening? I wanted so much to go into the bedroom and talk to Uncle

James, but I was afraid, too. It was as though the bedroom was one of those lonely secret rooms in a fairy story. I did go in, to take him tea, and he was awake and he looked at me, but he could not seem to speak.

We did not go to church today.

Later in the afternoon Mr. Boothroyd came to visit again. He brought a hamper of food from Mr. Flanagan.

When he left, Auntie Janet went in to see Uncle James and when she came back out she fell into pieces. "What can he hope to do with that poor mangled hand? What will happen to us?" Uncle James is not talking to Auntie either.

I am lying in bed with the last bit of candle burning. The train whistle is a sad sound tonight.

December 19

Dear Papa and Mama,

This morning Auntie Janet and I went back to work. Everything was the same, but different. Same mill bell, same Mill Street. Same yellow dog. Same Barney. Oh, what if Uncle James turns out like him? Same parade of people. But different. The bell was harsh, the dog made me sad and the people walked apart from us. Well, not Murdo and his parents, but the ones from the other rooms.

Auntie took my arm and kept me close to her. "They don't know what to say," she said. "Troubles make people shy."

Most same and different was the works of the mill. All those wheels and belts, levers and pulleys. It was the monster of my dreams, waiting for a moment's inattention, one slip, one mistake and it would attack. I remembered Murdo explaining it all to me, the power and cleverness of it, how it was a wonder almost as amazing as the human brain. This morning all I saw was a foul fiend, all teeth and claws, banging and screeching so that we could not think, so that it could get us.

In our spinning room everyone wanted to know the news of Uncle James. Most everyone was very kind and that made me want to cry. Except Mrs. Brown. She was angry. She said that it was all the fault of the owners. She said that if the floors were not all slick with machine oil and tufts of wool James would never have slipped and fallen into the belt. She is right. The mill floors are very slippery, especially if you wear shoes. I usually take my shoes off, to save them, and also not to slip. So Mrs. Brown is right and I would like to be angry along with her. I would like to blame someone. But I cannot find anger in me. Only a hollow place, ringed round with fear.

December 20

Dear Papa and Mama,

Auntie Janet and I have been rushing home at dinner to see Uncle. Today he was sitting asleep and Mungo was on his shoulder. When he woke up he did not pay him any heed, even when Mungo tried to lick his nose. Uncle seems to have gone away.

Auntie and I made some shortbread this evening.

December 21

Dear Papa and Mama,

Dr. Reeve came today and changed Uncle's dressing and taught Auntie how to make a sling for his arm. He says the healing is going well. He talked about the Christmas party, which is to be on Friday and we will all get off early. Auntie Janet made tea and chatted, but Uncle James hardly said a word. When the doctor said, "I hope we'll see you at the party, James, it would take your mind off things," he didn't even reply. I could tell that Auntie was ashamed for his rudeness.

December 22

Dear Papa and Mama,

Everyone at work is talking about the party. Auntie says that she cannot persuade Uncle James to go and so she won't leave him, but that I am to go.

Is this right? Should I stay home too? Is this a time when being obedient is the wrong thing to do? If I stayed home perhaps I could cheer Uncle up. They are starting a new story in the newspaper. I could read that. But I so want to go to the party. The wanting is as big as the sadness about the accident.

Uncle ate some supper tonight, but then he just wanted to sit and stare. I feel as though Auntie and I are twittering birds, talking around him. I think he is cross with us.

December 24

Dear Papa and Mama,

I did go to the party last night. The Campbells took me with them. It was grand, the best party I have ever been to. (I know. It is really the only party I have ever been to.) When I was getting ready to go (I wore my red Sunday dress) I got a bad feeling in my stomach because Uncle James and Auntie Janet were not coming. But Auntie Janet fixed my hair in a new way and told me to have a good time and she would be happy thinking of me.

When we got to the town hall my bad feeling dissolved because the first thing we saw was a huge Christmas tree, all decorated with candles and shiny ornaments. It was as tall as the ceiling and it smelled like the outdoors. Matron did not think

Christmas trees were necessary, so we never had one. On the top was a beautiful angel, dressed in a blue gown, with fluffy wings. I thought of you both in heaven and then I thought that maybe the baby Jesus was so fresh out of heaven that he brought a little taste of it with him when he came to earth. Maybe all babies do and that's why we are happy looking at them. Even if it does mean all those nappies and the crying and such. What did Mary and Joseph do about nappies? That might not be a proper question, but I do wonder because I washed a lot of nappies in the Home and I don't know how you would manage that if you were living in a stable.

Back to the party. Mr. Boothroyd played the fiddle and everyone was dancing. Just when my feet were so wanting to dance that they almost danced away by themselves, Bertha Rose whirled by and grabbed my hand. She said, "Let's show those clodhoppers how it's done." I don't know the first thing about dancing, but it was so crowded that nobody paid us any attention and we just whirled around and had a grand time. There was a great mix-up with something called a grand chain and then I ended up dancing with lots of other people, even ones I didn't know. It was very merry.

There was a big table covered with food and drinks. I had lemonade and ham sandwiches and then I danced more and had lemonade and cake and cookies and tea.

When Mr. Boothroyd took a rest some of the people got up and sang songs. Eddie McDougal, the bald man who works in the dye shed, had a voice that filled the whole room. He sang a Scottish song called "The Road to the Isles." One of the lines of the song is, "Their laughter puts the leap upon the lame." That line went round and round in my head all evening, like the mill wheel.

I got to talking with a girl who works over at Big Red. She asked me if I knew what they said about the long underwear they make. I said no and she said, "It is so itchy that it tickles your fancy." Then we both got the giggles.

At the end of the evening Mr. Flanagan and his wife gave out the presents that were under the tree. We all opened them on the spot. Mine is a pink hankie with lace, the prettiest I have ever had. I don't think I will ever blow my nose on it, but will save it to dab my fevered brow, if ever I have a fevered brow. And we each got a bag of ribbon candy.

When I got home Uncle James had gone to bed, but Auntie Janet and I sat up and I told her all about it. We ate ribbon candy and Mungo played with the bag.

Today I found a good Christmas present for Auntie Janet.

Christmas Day
Afternoon
Dear Papa and Mama,

Auntie and Uncle have gone for a walk. We all had a lie-in this morning as we were late last night after the midnight service. Yesterday Uncle James said he was not going to come to church and Auntie Janet got very angry and said that he had to come. I have never seen her angry before and I hope she is never that angry at me. But he agreed to come. Church was grand, full to the very edges of the pews. We sang "Silent Night," "Hark the Herald Angels Sing," "Good King Wenceslas" and "O Come, All Ye Faithful."

There was the crèche with the Holy Family and the shepherds and wise men and animals. There was a crèche in the church in Kingston too. It used to make me sad because it was such a happy family. I used to think that having a family was "happily ever after." This year I know that having a family is just the beginning of the story. This year I know about different kinds of sad.

In "O Come, All Ye Faithful" it says, "Sing, all ye citizens of heaven above," and I imagined that you were singing with me.

The singing was so loud that my own voice was just woven into the whole sound. I like that. Uncle James was next to me and he didn't sing.

When the service finished, Rev. Parfitt stood at the door of the church and shook our hands. "Merry Christmas, Flora," he said to me. It came to my mind how many grown-up people know my name here in Almonte. Rev. and Mrs. Parfitt, Murdo's parents, Granny Whitall, Mr. Haskin and Mrs. Murphy and Mrs. Brown and Fred and all the other people at the mill. When I lived in the Home only Matron and Cook and a few other grown-ups knew my name. I am more of a person in Almonte than I was before.

Walking home, the snow was blowing and Auntie Janet said it was the rude wind's wild lament and that gave us the notion to sing "Good King Wenceslas" just by ourselves. We tried to get Uncle James to sing the king part, but he wouldn't. So we made our voices deep and did it ourselves.

Then we had presents. Auntie and Uncle gave me a new notebook, as I have nearly finished this one, even with writing small. All those clean white pages, and a stiff green mottled cover. I gave Uncle James his socks and he did thank me, but Auntie Janet had to suggest that he try them on. I gave Auntie Janet a pair of scissors shaped like a bird, just like the ones the lady on the train had. They have a little blue velvet case. Auntie Janet cried.

December 26
Boxing Day
Dear Papa and Mama,

Yesterday Auntie and I had dinner with the Campbell family. We went down in the morning to help. I have not mentioned this before, but Mrs. Campbell is expecting another baby. Auntie helped Mrs. Campbell and Kathleen with the cooking and Murdo and I took the little ones outside to play. We made a snow fort and had a great battle. I pretended that I was being helpful, keeping the little ones out of the way, but really I was throwing snowballs as hard as I could and yelling loud just for me. It felt grand. Sometimes I tire of being good.

When we came in, everything smelled wonderful, of turkey and mincemeat.

Auntie and I went upstairs to get our chairs and Uncle, but he refused to come for dinner. The sad place in my stomach that the snowball fight had dissolved came back again. Finally Auntie just took him a plate.

When Mr. Campbell was serving the turkey he asked me if I wanted the parson's nose. Everyone groaned and giggled and then Mrs. Campbell said, "Oh, Donald, quit with your teasing," and Kathleen took pity on me and explained that the parson's nose is the, well, rude end of the turkey and of course I didn't want it. I must remember this for next Christmas.

We ate until we could eat no more and then we found a little place in our stomachs for shortbread.

I took some scraps of turkey for Mungo, who could hardly eat for purring.

December 27

Dear Papa and Mama,

I cannot write very much. I just want to put my head under the covers and go to sleep. Uncle James went back to work today. Mr. Flanagan has given him a job sweeping. I was hoping that he would be happier. Not at all. When he came home he was in a very dark mood. No matter what kind and cheerful thing Auntie Janet said, he would not answer, and then he started yelling — that he was useless, like an old shoddy rag that should just be thrown into the rag-grinder. While he was in the middle of yelling, a train came by. I have never liked that noise so much because it drowned him out.

December 28

Dear Papa and Mama,

Mr. Flanagan opened the slide again today and I went along with Murdo and Kathleen after work. But it was not as much fun without Auntie and

Uncle. Also it is much colder than it was. The air hurts. I went on one run, then I left the toboggan for the others and came home.

December 30

Dear Papa and Mama,

I am angry at Uncle James. There. I have said it. I know it is wicked to be angry with him. I know his arm and hand pain him and he is sad because he cannot weave. I know he is disappointed about his dreams to become a loom fixer. I know he is vexed about money. I know all these things, but I am still angry. He is so grumpy and he does not think anything is good and he seems to want Auntie Janet and me to feel this way too. He does not want us to be happy.

Like this evening. After supper Auntie and I were remembering about Miss Beulah Young and the Temperance lecture. We found that we remembered that song about belonging and we started to sing it.

Then Auntie began to tease Uncle that he had never signed the pledge and all of a sudden he exploded. He said it was all nonsense, that working men had little enough pleasure in their lives, and who was some silly, privileged spinster to tell them that they mustn't drink. I started to tell him that she wasn't rich, that she was a half-orphan. Auntie tried to tell him that Miss Beulah Young talked about how there needed to be cozy clubs for working men to go instead of taverns, so they could improve themselves. But Uncle James wasn't listening. He said that getting people all excited to sign the pledge was wicked, because they had no intention of keeping that promise and then that turned them into liars. Uncle James was practically yelling. I don't understand. It is not as if Uncle James even goes to the tavern. I felt light as a bird when Auntie and I were singing and now I feel squashed.

1888

January 1, 1888

Dear Papa and Mama,

Two things about 1888. Murdo-who-knows-everything says that it has been one thousand years since there was a year with so many 8s in it. And 1888 will be a leap year. The last time there was a February 29 I was eight years old, but I do not remember it.

Last night was Hogmanay, the end of the old year and the beginning of the new. We stayed up until midnight to welcome in the new year. Auntie Janet said that we had to do first footing. I had never heard of this, but she said her Grandma Dow taught it to her. First footing is when the first person to come in your door in the new year must be a tall man with black hair, so that you have good luck the year through.

Of course it should have been Uncle James, since he is tall and dark, but he said it was nonsense, and then Auntie Janet asked him if it was nonsense then why had he done it last year. And then he said well what good luck had the year held?

Then there was a long silence and Auntie said, "It brought us Flora, James." And then he just walked away.

I expected Auntie Janet to give up then, but she just set her mouth firm and went downstairs and asked Arthur Whitall to do it. He is not very tall and not very dark, but at least he is a man.

Arthur Whitall turned out to be a very good sport. One of the things about first footing is that the first footer has to leave the house by one door and come in by another, but the building only has one outside door. So Arthur agreed to climb out the Campbells' window and then come in by the front door.

So a few minutes before midnight he climbed out the window. Percy and Archie found this the funniest thing they had ever seen. Then right after midnight there was a loud knocking. We went and welcomed him in and Auntie whispered the good luck poem to him, line by line, and he repeated it in a good loud voice.

Good luck to the house
Good luck to the family.
Good luck to every rafter of it.
And to every worldly thing in it.
Good luck to the good-wife,
Good luck to the children.
Good luck to every friend
Good fortune and health to all.

Then Mr. Whitall and Mr. Campbell all had a drink of whisky and so did Mrs. Campbell and Granny Whitall, but not Auntie Janet because of the pledge.

We kept the fire alight all night for good luck.

January 2

Dear Papa and Mama,

Back to work. My mind wanders a good deal of the time when I am at work. The sound of the machinery has a rhythm to it and it as though my body stays in the mill, doffing, but my mind walks out the door and down and street and out of town and into the woods where the fairies are. Doffing and piecing take noticing, but not much thinking. This morning the snow was coming down in huge soft flakes and I had time to stare out the window, following one flake as it danced down to the ground. I turned into a fairy, riding a snowflake like riding a horse, or sailing in a snowflake boat. As a fairy I was all wrapped in white furs and I was toasty warm with a fur muff for my hands. When I am a fairy in the spring I sew new leaves to the trees. In the summer I spin and weave the clouds into a lovely cape for the fairy queen. In the fall all the fairies fly out on the night of the huge harvest moon with our tiny vats of dye (they are really walnut shells) and dye the trees crimson and orange. When humans see us they think we are fireflies.

I give a good deal of thought to fairies. I would like to tell Ann about the fairies, but she would say that fairies are not real and snow is just snow.

Uncle James has stopped going to work. He says that sweeping is a job for boys.

January 3

Dear Papa and Mama,

Here is something that I cannot tell anyone but you. I cannot bear to look at Uncle James's hand. It is so ugly, pink and shiny like Crazy Barney's arm. I know this is shameful. I would like to be like Mungo, who treats Uncle James just as he used to. But I cannot.

January 4

Dear Papa and Mama,

Uncle James has stopped shaving. He cannot do it himself and he won't let Auntie help him. Perhaps when he has a real beard it will be fine, but now he just looks like a tramp. I think back to when I first came to Almonte and we all joked about men with beards. It seems like a long time ago.

January 5

Dear Papa and Mama,

I'm writing this at the rectory. This evening, Auntie and I were invited to visit Mrs. Parfitt. Uncle James was invited, but he would not come. It was good to get out of the house. Uncle James is like a heavy dark cloud in the corner. Auntie Janet took some mending to do and I took this book. There is a lovely warm fire and Mrs. Parfitt is boiling the water for tea. I'm on a low stool and Robbie, a friendly wheezy old dog, is sitting on my feet. Auntie and Mrs. Parfitt are talking of this and that. I am half-listening.

I had a thought about Mrs. Parfitt. Up until now I thought that she was just being kind to us because she is the minister's wife and she is obliged to be kind to everyone in the church and help them out in their troubles. But looking at Auntie Janet and Mrs. Parfitt talking, I can see that they are more like friends. They are both younger than most of the church ladies (and prettier).

Pause for listening.

Here I am, back again. When I heard the word *Flanagan* I started to listen more than half. Mrs. Parfitt told Auntie Janet that Mr. Flanagan is trying to divorce his wife. She said the word *divorce* in a very quiet way. Then her voice got even quieter and she said that on weekends "fancy ladies" come up on the train from Toronto to visit Mr. Flanagan. I didn't know what this meant, but Auntie Janet gasped. So I made the mistake of looking up, and then they remembered me and then they stopped talking. Mrs. Parfitt said, "Little pitchers." I know what this means. It means "Little pitchers have big ears," and it means don't talk about this in front of the children. They changed the subject to plans for the church concert. This made me very cross. I am not a child. I am an employee of the Almonte Woollen Mill and if I don't know what a fancy lady is I should be able to ask. Of course I *don't.*

The tea is ready. I wonder if there will be biscuits.

January 7

Dear Papa and Mama,

Payday today. When we got home Uncle James was out. He sometimes goes for long tramps on his own. Auntie Janet boiled the kettle for tea and then she noticed that there was no tea left and she started to cry. I said I would go along to the store, which stays open on the nights of payday, but she said that if we bought tea we mightn't be able to pay the rent. Then she said that she is lying awake in the night fretting about how we can afford to live with Uncle James not working.

I remembered a treat that Cook once made for me and I put milk and sugar into two cups and filled them with boiling water and said to Auntie Janet that we would have fairy tea. That made her cry all the more. I know about that kind of crying. When you're so sad that you think you cannot bear it and somebody is kind to you, you just turn into a wet thing. But then she stopped and dabbed her eyes and even smiled a bit. Auntie Janet is a pretty crier. I am a horrid crier. My nose runs, my eyes get red, my face gets blotchy. Perhaps I will be a pretty crier too when I grow up.

After tea I got the idea that Auntie Janet and I needed to do sums. At the Home the girls did not learn arithmetic, but I was always helping the boys with their school work so I got good at doing sums. I made Auntie Janet put her pay on the table and I did the same. I had $1.60 and she had $4.65. So that made $6.25. Our rent is $1.90. We spend $1 a week on wood and candles. This leaves us $3.35 a week for food. She says that she spends $5 a week for food and then she started to get glum again, but I said we could look at what we could do without. We looked at everything we had eaten all week — bread, butter, tea, bacon, beans, coffee, oatmeal, potato, turnip, cheese, sugar, flour, treacle, milk. We figured that we could manage without coffee and cheese and bacon and that fairy tea would be fine until Uncle James got well again. We can also save on candles because Auntie knows so many stories and you don't need light to tell tales. We finished the evening with the tale of a wizard who knew "black magic and white magic and the whole of the shades between."

We went to bed much comforted, but as I write this (by moonlight; what will I do when it is new moon?) I have two more thoughts. One is that I wonder if Uncle James will ever be able to go back to work. The other is that our sums did not include laundry or church collection and what about clothes? I know what Auntie would say: Don't creep up on trouble lest trouble creep up on you.

January 10

Dear Papa and Mama,

It is terribly cold. Thirty degrees below zero. Auntie wrapped newspapers around my chest before I put on my dress this morning. I sound crinkly and

I am a funny lumpy shape, but it did help to keep warm on the walk to the mill. But coming home was a misery. It felt as though all the warm damp air inside me froze to hard crystals as soon as I stepped out the mill door. Mrs. Brown said that she was almost hoping that the river would freeze and close the mill. But Mr. Lewis said that the Mississippi has never frozen solid. And then Mr. Wyley said that his grandfather remembered a year when it froze for a whole month and then there was a great discussion about whose grandfather remembered what. Anyway, I certainly hope the mill does not close, because we need our wages.

January 12

Dear Papa and Mama,

Today began well and ended badly. It is still bitter cold. The railway is buried in drifts ten feet deep. And the mill did close. So Uncle James and Murdo and Mr. Campbell and some of the other men borrowed a horse and sleigh to go ice fishing. Auntie and I spent the day close to the stove, mending and knitting. It was very hard to keep warm even wrapped in blankets — the wind was blowing snow against the windows and they let in great drafts, even stuffed at the edges with *The Almonte Gazette.* We agreed that we would rather be at the mill, because at least it would be warm.

But then Mrs. Campbell came in with the little ones. Mrs. Campbell is very large. The baby must be coming soon. Auntie began to tell stories and soon we forgot our chilly toes and numb fingers. She told the story of the bride and the water kelpie. She said the story was for me because it is about a weaver's daughter. This daughter never speaks, but she catches the eye of a travelling soldier and he marries her because she has hair like the wing of a blackbird and eyes as blue as flax flowers. As soon as Auntie started to talk about romance, Percy and Archie began to giggle. It turns out that the weaver's girl is bewitched by a water kelpie and that is why she does not speak. Then the soldier goes to an old wise woman for advice and she says that the girl must do this and that to remove the spell and she does and then she can talk. But then the problem is that she can't stop talking, clackiting all the day long.

When Auntie got to this part in the story, Mrs. Campbell said, "Well, we know a few like that, don't we?" and then they fell to giggling before Auntie Janet got back to the story. So the young woman and the water kelpie had a talking contest and they both tired themselves out and from then on the young woman talked neither too much nor too little, but just the right amount. And they made the wise woman the godmother to their first-born child. What we learn from the story is not to go out in the gloaming or drink from the fairy well. (Or talk too much?)

We were all happy, thinking about the story and talking about talking, too much and too little. Then the men came home, half-frozen, but merry because they had caught, between them, seventy-six eels! Uncle James seemed to have woken up, to be his old self again.

This is where the day started to go wrong. Auntie Janet and Mrs. Campbell said we should cook some of the eels right away and all eat together. I helped skin and gut them. You have to make a slit around the base of the neck and try to pull the skin off like a glove, but they are slippery, and I started to feel so ill. The worst thing was the smell — horrid, very strong and sweet. We cut them into pieces and then Auntie put them with water in a dish in the oven. When it came time to eat them I just could not. My stomach was turning over just at the thought of them. I could not stop myself from thinking they were large worms. And Uncle James was peeved with me because I would not even try. So I did try and then I vomited. And then Auntie Janet was cross with Uncle James and the Campbells all went home and I am so ashamed.

January 15

Dear Papa and Mama,

Usually Sunday lunch is my favourite meal of the week, but today we did not have very much, and Auntie tried to pretend that she wasn't hungry, and that made Uncle angry. I am filled with sadness. Also fear. This morning I came upon Auntie trying to line her shoes with scraps of leather. But it was no good. They are too far gone to be mended. "I can tie string around them," she said, "but I can't go to church like that." Then she said that she could borrow Uncle's boots and then we both started to laugh at the thought of her clumping along in Uncle's huge boots and then the laughing turned into crying.

Then she talked and talked, saying how many plans she and Uncle James had had, and how they were so excited that I was to come and live with them, and how it had all become so hard and perhaps they should never have taken me away from the Home. I was just holding my breath, thinking she was going to say that I must go back, but she did not say that. Will she?

We did not go to church.

Mungo is pushing his nose into my hand, which means he wants petting.

January 19

Dear Papa and Mama,

This is the saddest I have been in Almonte. Uncle James is in a rage. He has stormed out of the house. Auntie Janet is crying. It is all because Auntie suggested that he write to his brother in British Columbia to ask for help.

Uncle James says that Auntie Janet is trying to humiliate him and that he will not ask for charity. This does not make any sense. Auntie Janet and I cannot earn enough to keep us all. Already we owe money at the store, and how will we pay it? Why is Uncle James acting like this? Surely it is not charity when it is your own brother. Or is this something I do not know about families?

And even if it is charity, what about St. Paul? "And now abideth faith, hope and charity, these three; but the greatest of these is charity."

January 20

Dear Papa and Mama,

The mill is open again and Auntie and I are back at work. I am glad to be there because it is warm and the clatter drowns out my thoughts.

January 21

Dear Papa and Mama,

Uncle took the splint off his arm today. The stitches are gone and it looks better, but he can't bend it straight at the elbow. He wears a glove on his hand, even indoors.

It was a payday without much pay. When we got home we discovered that Mr. Boothroyd had been by and dropped off another hamper of food from Mr. Flanagan. There was tea and bacon. Auntie Janet nearly cried and then she said how kind Mr. Flanagan was and that set Uncle off again in a rage talking about Mr. Flanagan sitting around in his huge warm house, making a fortune from our work, and tossing us crumbs. Then he went off somewhere.

Mrs. Parfitt came by this evening with a pair of shoes that she said she could not wear because they pinched her feet and she just wondered if they might fit Auntie Janet. She said that she bought them a size too small through vanity, but that Auntie Janet had lovely small feet and it would be a favour to her if they could be used, rather than sitting in the cupboard looking accusing.

They did fit.

I can see that kindness is a very complicated matter.

Later I asked Auntie if Uncle wouldn't notice that

she had new shoes and she said no, that he is not noticing very much about her these days.

January 22

Dear Papa and Mama,

It is late afternoon. I am having a cup of human (not fairy) tea and I smell beans and bacon cooking. My heart is lighter. Here is why:

Auntie and I went to church this morning, but not Uncle. Rev. Parfitt preached a very long sermon. Miss Steele and Miss Steele started to nod off. All of the Campbells except Kathleen started to fidget. I lost track of what he was saying and began to look through the hymn book. I never thought about this before, but those hymn writers knew about troubles. They write a lot about fathers in distress and our feeble frame and how we are frail as summer's flower and the elements madly around us raging. In the hymns there is always an answer to these troubles, but this morning I could not think of any answer to ours.

It was cold, but sunny, and after church Auntie said did I want to walk around to the other side of the river. There was something different about her. I thought it was maybe just the new shoes, but it wasn't. As we walked she told me that she had a plan, but she needed my help. She needed me to help her write a letter. "We can't go on this way," she said. "We have to tell James's brother how things are with us, but we need to do it without James knowing."

So we went home. Uncle James was off somewhere, on one of his tramps, so all afternoon we have worked on a letter. In it we tell Wilfred Duncan about Uncle's accident and how he can only do sweeping at the mill. We talked for a long time about how to describe the way he is and finally we decided on "ailing in spirit." We asked if Wilfred had any ideas of what we might do. And then we said that James did not know we had written this letter and he must never find out. It took us all afternoon to write the letter, but when we were done I felt like I had sunlight for my load. Auntie said that troubles shared are troubles halved. I will mail the letter tomorrow.

January 25

Dear Papa and Mama,

There is new operative in our room. Her name is Lillie Wyatt. She is twenty years old. She comes from a farm out near Pakenham. She has a sad story. Just before Christmas, her father was walking home from a neighbour's and he lost his way and froze to death. Her mother and brothers are carrying on with the farm, but they need money, so she has come to work in the mill. She is boarding with a family up in Irishtown.

When I heard this story it made me want to say to Uncle James that he should stop being so gloomy. At least he isn't dead. But I know this isn't fair. When you're sad it does not make you feel one bit better to hear of other people who are worse off than you. It should, but it doesn't.

Lillie Wyatt seems a shy, quiet sort of person, or perhaps she just hasn't been that much in company. At the dinner break she asked me if it is always this loud. I said yes, but you get used to it. I introduced her to Smokey. I remember how strange everything seemed to me when I began. Here is something odd: It seems almost forever since I was at the Home, but it does not seem that long that I have been in Almonte.

January 26

Dear Papa and Mama,

Murdo, who does not tire of reminding us that his father knows the cousin of the County Constable, came up at the dinner break today to tell us that there was a dangerous maniac in the Almonte Jail yesterday and that last night he tried to dig his way out and now he has been taken to Ottawa. This was a very unsatisfactory story because we don't know:

1. What does a "dangerous maniac" mean? What did he do to be put in jail?
2. What did he use to try to dig his way out?
3. How far did he get before he was discovered?

I know if Kathleen had not been hanging around, Murdo would have just invented the answers to these questions. Kathleen is far too keen on facts.

January 28

Dear Papa and Mama,

Today there was an eclipse of the moon. The sky was clear, so we could see it very well. By six o'clock the moon had completely disappeared and then it started to come back, first of all just a rim of light and then bigger and bigger. It went from a new moon to a full moon in just one hour.

I wish time would really speed up like that so we would get a reply to our letter. Every day I think about the letter, on the train across Canada. I think about how fast the train goes. I know it is too soon for a reply from Wilfred Duncan, but I hope anyway. If he answers right away, that could mean that he cannot help. But if he waits too long to reply, it could mean the same thing. This is like waiting for the next part of the story in the newspaper. All week long you try to guess what will happen.

February 5

Dear Papa and Mama,

I have not written in a week because I have been ailing. On Monday I woke up with knives in my throat. Even porridge hurt. But I did not say anything because I did not want to worry Auntie Janet. Then as we began work I felt hotter and hotter and my legs didn't work very well. Then I fainted.

Mr. Haskin let Auntie Janet have an hour off to take me home. At first I was so happy just to be lying down, but I started to feel worse and worse. Granny Whitall brought me tea, but I couldn't eat anything. The days and nights got all mixed up and so did my thinking. I got words in my head and I couldn't get them out. Words like *the wicked wizard of Mischanter Hill.* The words didn't mean anything, but I kept thinking them over and over again, as though the next time I thought them they would mean something important. Then I got a wee bit better and started to fret about losing my wages. Auntie told me that Mr. Flanagan was keeping my job for me, so that was kind.

One good thing about being sick was that Uncle James went back to work. He can take his bad arm out of the sling for a few hours at a time. He is still gloomy.

But now I am well again and will return to the mill tomorrow.

February 6

Dear Papa and Mama,

Today I came across Mr. Longfellow's poem. I had forgotten about it. There is one last verse:

And the night shall be filled with music
And the cares, that infest the day,
Shall fold their tents, like the Arabs,
And as silently steal away.

February 9

Dear Papa and Mama,

Uncle does not seem to listen when I read the newspaper to him, except when something makes him angry. But I read it anyway and try to figure out what might make him angry and I don't read those parts. Today I read about a trapper who caught a forty-eight-pound beaver. And how in a place called Ohio they dug up a grave and found out that the woman in the grave had turned completely to stone except for her feet. This is called "petrification." It took ten men to lift the body.

Then there was something quite mysterious right in Almonte. Uncle didn't care, but Auntie and I wondered about it: *A young woman has appeared twice at the skating rink in male attire and she is promised a visit to the magistrate if she repeats the performance.*

February 10

Dear Papa and Mama,

No letter. Auntie says it is still too soon to get our hopes up. But my hopes are already up.

February 11

Dear Papa and Mama,

Today Uncle James and I were walking along the railway tracks and we saw two little boys jumping out of a slowly moving stock car onto the snowy slope beside the rail, and then sliding down. Uncle just roared over and grabbed them both and gave them a loud talking-to. He used some words that I will not write here, but mostly he asked them what they thought would happen if they slipped and rolled onto the track. Uncle James is fearsome when he is angry and both boys were speechless and unmoving. I think you could say they were petrified. Then Uncle made them tell him their names and where they lived and he went off with them, holding them by their ears.

I went back home alone, thinking two thoughts. Sometimes being angry is a good thing. And Uncle scooped up both those boys like someone with two strong arms. He must be getting better.

February 12

Dear Papa and Mama,

Today we had Psalm 148. This is the one where everybody gets in on the praising and it is one of my favourite bits of the Bible. I think this means that we will have good news this week.

February 13

Dear Papa and Mama,

Oh ye spindles and bobbins, boots and bacon, mosquitoes and maniacs, turtles and toboggans, praise ye the Lord! Praise him and magnify him forever! The letter has come.

This evening I started to read the paper aloud when Uncle James pulled a letter out of his pocket. "Could you read this instead?" he said. He was trying to look as though he didn't much care about it, but I could tell he was curious.

"It is from Wilfred Duncan," I said. "Yes," he answered, "I could tell that much. We already had his letter, didn't we? What's he doing writing again so soon?"

Auntie Janet and I did not look at one another.

I read the letter. It started out from his wife Nellie. She said that the town where they live has a chance of getting a school if they have ten children to attend. But they only have nine in the town.

"Unless someone moves here we'll have to wait two years for Joseph to reach school age before we can have a school. I was delighted, therefore, to hear your good news of Flora. If you were to move here and be with us we could get a school." Then she said how she has been lonely for family and company. She said that the children are lovely, but too small for a good conversation.

Then Wilfred took over the letter. He said that he had 130 head of cattle and was looking to expand by getting more land, but that it was very difficult to get good help. He said that he remembered how good James was with animals, even when he was just a boy, and he needed a reliable, hard-working man that he could count on. He said he realized that James probably had his own plans, but would he at least consider a move, because the future lay in the west.

There was more about building us a cabin and how they were only twelve miles from Kamloops, which was a fine place. He ended the letter saying that he would have no peace from Nellie until there was a school, and of course James knew what wives are like when they get an idea in their heads.

The letter did not give one hint of our having written him about Uncle James's injury. That Wilfred Duncan must be not only kind, but clever with it.

When I finished reading, there was a long pause. I did not dare look at Auntie Janet. I don't think that either of us imagined such a big idea.

But when I looked at Uncle James I could see right away that it was good. There was a real person looking out of his eyes. He was the first to speak.

"What do you think?" he said. "Are you ready to be a pioneer in the wild west?" Auntie Janet did not even pause. She just smiled and said, "Whither thou goest." I knew this meant yes because it is in the Bible, "Whither thou goest I will go."

Then Uncle James did the most amazing thing. He turned to me and asked if I was willing to move west. Nobody has ever asked me such a thing, if I was willing to go here or there. I was so surprised that I could not say anything from the Bible or anything at all so I just nodded.

Then he looked at Auntie Janet in a way that made me think it would be a good thing for me to come down and thread some needles for Granny Whitall, which is where I am now, writing by the light of her candle.

February 14

Dear Papa and Mama,

Today I nearly fell asleep while doffing. Last night I could not sleep for excitement and this morning I read the letter aloud again and we talked about all our questions. Did they have a garden? Auntie Janet hopes so. Are there animals other than horses and cattle? Uncle James hopes so. We talked so much we were nearly late for work.

After supper Uncle James had me write a letter accepting the invitation and saying we would come as soon as we could give notice at the mill and arrange our travel.

Thoughts pop into my mind that could be worries. What will school be like? What will it be like living out in the bush? (Is it bush?) Will there be wild animals? Will I have to take care of the children? (Nappies and dripping noses, crying and tempers.) But, strange to say, none of these are really worries. Why not? Because I could go anywhere with Auntie and Uncle and it would still be home. A family is like a home that you can pick up and carry with you. So that's one more thing to add to my list of what I know about families. They tease. They don't give up easily. They ask each other before they make decisions. You can take them with you.

I wonder if Auntie Janet will ever tell Uncle James about our letter. Maybe when they are as old as Granny Whitall. Or maybe never. Maybe that is one more thing I know about families. Sometimes they have kind secrets.

Mungo is pushing the pencil out of my hand. That means, "Stop writing. It is time for bed." He is probably right.

Epilogue

With much regret Flora agreed that it was not possible to take Mungo on the trip west. She gave him to Lillie, who spoiled him just as much as Flora had. He made the most of his nine lives and lived to be seventeen years old.

Upon their arrival in British Columbia, Flora's family got suddenly much bigger. The Wilfred Duncans had five children, and late in 1888 Janet had the first of what would be four children of her own. Flora's world was rich in cousins and she ended up with as much family as anyone could want.

Murdo and his family stayed on at the mill in Almonte. One of the room supervisors noticed Murdo's engineering interests and recommended him for further training. By eighteen Murdo was a mill mechanic — a job he kept his whole working life. With such a wide country between them, though, the Campbells and the Duncans eventually lost touch.

Life on the ranch turned out to be hard work. Uncle James worked with the cattle and horses. Wilfred said that he believed that James spoke horse and cow. James's disabled hand made some jobs more difficult, but he always said that if he had ten fingers he would still be weaving his life away. Auntie Janet had to learn many new skills, such as canning and the care of chickens.

And life in the west did not mean the end of child labour. Some days, what with gardening, cooking, washing and child-minding, Flora worked every bit as hard and as long as she had in the mill, but there were three big differences. The first was that the work varied with the seasons. Sometimes it was very busy, but often there was time for lots of fun — Flora never lost her love of the "tobog" and she learned to play the mandolin. The second difference was that their hard work resulted in rewards they could see, improvements to the ranch and to their shared lives. The third difference was that Flora had a chance to go to school. She went right through high school and was the first graduate of the school she helped make possible.

Flora married at age eighteen — a young man who was kind, responsible and could sing the birds out of the trees. He had the extravagant first name of Ulysses, which meant that the apple peeling had been right. He worked in the general store in Kamloops and eventually took over the business. By the time Canada celebrated Queen Victoria's Diamond Jubilee in 1897, Flora had two babies, and by the new century she was the mother of four. Flora and Ulysses settled permanently in Kamloops, building a house, raising a family, running a business and weaving a life.

Flora's children often helped in the store after school. Sometimes, if they wanted to play hockey or go fishing instead, they complained. Flora, who was a no-nonsense mother, always answered by telling them that if they wanted to know what hard work was, they should have worked in a mill. The children listened politely to their mother's stories of the olden days, but really they preferred her stories of princesses and fairies, stories she had learned from her Auntie Janet and told over and over again by the fire on cold winter nights or sitting by the river in summer.

When Auntie Janet left the mill she took with her a bag of wool scraps from the mungo barrel. During the first winter in the west she and Flora cut and pieced and made a quilt from the scraps. It was not beautiful, as the colours were mostly dark blues, browns and greys, but it was warm and durable. Over the years, as it became worn, Flora would mend it, and as she sewed she would think back to the brief chapter in her life when she was a doffer, a piecer, and an Almonter — the chapter in which she first found a family.

Historical Note

When we look into the past, the most interesting times are those when things were changing. Flora grew up in a time of change. There were new technologies, with great excitement about the uses for electricity, the invention of the telephone and the mechanization of work. The way people talked about the machines in mills, for example, is like the way we talk about computers. A nineteenth-century writer said of these machines, "Their ingenuity seems not only to supplant human intelligence, but to surpass it."

Ideas were also changing. In the late 1800s, people were questioning religious beliefs, the role of women, how wealth was distributed in society and how children should be treated. In our time and place we think that the "job" of children is to go to school and to play. In Flora's time, many people felt that it was right and proper that children should work for ten hours a day, six days a week, in mills and factories, in dangerous, unhealthy, tedious, ill-paid jobs. But the winds of change were blowing. Social reformers were asking society to take a look at the conditions of labour, and of child labour in particular.

By the time Flora went to Almonte, there were laws against children working. Basically, boys under twelve and girls under fourteen were not supposed to be employed. But these laws were not well enforced, and when Canadian federal commissioners toured the country in 1887 looking at working conditions, they found children working in a huge variety of jobs. They found children in factories — making boxes, cigars, nails, shoes, wire, starch, biscuits and matches. They found children in ironworks, bakeries, retail shops, printers, sugar refineries and sawmills. Most of all, they found children employed in textile mills.

The conditions under which these children worked were dangerous and unhealthy in many ways. Loud, continuous noise damaged hearing. Fibres floating in the air caused lung problems. Long hours of work, often in cramped conditions, hampered the development of healthy bones and posture. Workplace safety was often neglected and industrial accidents involving the loss of fingers and toes were not uncommon. Some mill bosses simply did not care. In 1887 a mill commissioner asked, "Is there anything which protects the children when they are around the machines?" The supervisor replied, "No; there's nothing. Each one has his work to do and if he does not protect himself, so much the worse for him."

Those in favour of the employment of children — which included, of course, those who used them as a cheap source of labour — made three main arguments. The first was practical. They asked, "If children were not working, what would they do? They would be out on the streets getting into trouble." The second argument was economic. Factory and mill owners and investors maintained that if they had to pay adult wages for all their labour, they could not make enough money. This argument was also used by the workers themselves. Many families could not survive on the wages of the adults — they needed the children's wages. The third argument was moral. Work was seen as a moral good, instilling a sense of responsibility in children and saving them from the sin of idleness.

Reformers realized that child labour could not simply be abolished. That change had to go hand in hand with the development of public education and with improvements in wages and working conditions, such as safety regulations and sick leave, so that a man and his wife could raise a family without putting their children to work.

The report of the commissioners who came to Almonte made clear and firm recommendations about child labour: *We are firmly persuaded that the continuous employment of children under fourteen should be forbidden. Such prohibition we believe essential to proper physical development and the securing of an ordinary education. Further, medical testimony proves conclusively that girls, when approaching womanhood, cannot be employed at severe or long-continued work without serious danger to their health, and the evil effects may follow them throughout their lives.*

Official reports such as these played a role in achieving reforms, but it takes more than recommendations and laws to make people change their minds and hearts.

Reformers used cartoons and poetry to rally support for their cause and to tweak the conscience of those in power. Poet Ernest Crosby imagined factory machines devouring children:

What are the machines saying? They are saying,
We are hungry. We have eaten up the men
and women (there is no longer a market for
men and women, they come too high) —
We have eaten up the men and women, and now
we are devouring the boys and girls.
How good they taste as we suck the blood from
their rounded cheeks and forms, and cast
them aside sallow and thin and care-worn,
and then call for more.

Sarah Nordcliffe Cleghorn, writing in the 1900s, used a simpler and more sarcastic approach:

The golf links lie so near the mill,
That almost every day,

The laboring children can look out,
And watch the men at play.

Journalists created emotion-filled word pictures to reveal the effects of child labour: *The cotton mill produces a type that can't be mistaken anywhere. An under-sized boy, a narrow chest, a shifting and uncertain gait, an expressionless face, and a soul that hopes not, for there is nought in the cotton mill worker's life but the long hours of toil, repulsive food, bare walls, and at the close a hole in the ground.*

One of the most powerful tools that reformers used was photography. In the early part of the twentieth century, a New York schoolteacher and photographer named Lewis Hine went about the United States taking photos of children working. His stunning pictures of ragged, grubby, stalwart children — photos identified with plain, factual captions — played a huge role in the abolishment of child labour. Gradually the laws came to be enforced and children disappeared from the workforce, at least officially.

Child labour reform was one of the great accomplishments of the time in which Flora lived, but the challenge remains. In our time it is estimated that over two hundred and fifty million children under the age of fourteen are employed around the world, many in extremely hazardous environments.

An organization called Human Rights Watch reports some of the worst stories: *Working at rug looms has left children disabled with eye damage, lung disease, stunted growth, and a susceptibility to arthritis as they grow older. Children making silk thread in India dip their hands into boiling water that burns and blisters them, breathe smoke and fumes from machinery, handle dead worms that cause infections, and guide twisting threads that cut their fingers. Children harvesting sugar cane in El Salvador use machetes to cut cane for up to nine hours a day in the hot sun; injuries to their hands and legs are common and medical care is often not available.*

The forces of reform are again at work. In many cases, young people are at the forefront of change. Canadian activist Craig Kielburger started an organization called Free The Children when he was just twelve years old. This organization continues to be a highly effective tool for education and change, working for a world in which all children can be safe and healthy, in which they can be free to learn and play.

Almonte’s No. 1 Mill was one of the leading woollen mills in Canada in the 1880s.

The churning falls on the Ottawa Valley's Mississippi River powered Almonte No. 1 Mill.

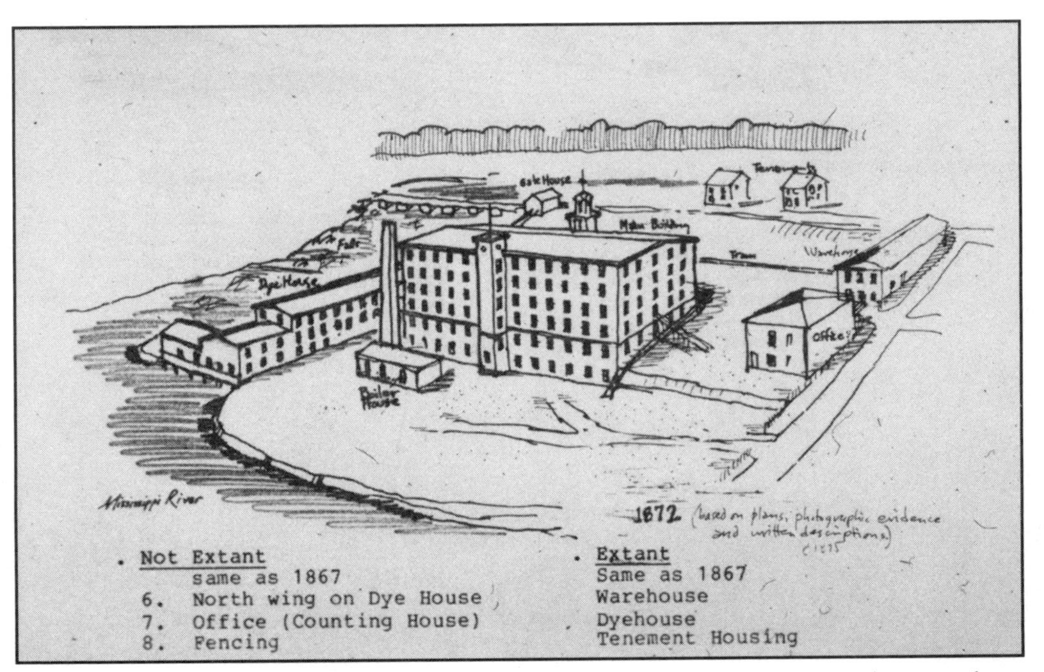

A layout of Almonte No. 1 Mill, showing the warehouses, dye houses, counting house and tenement housing for the workers, as of 1872.

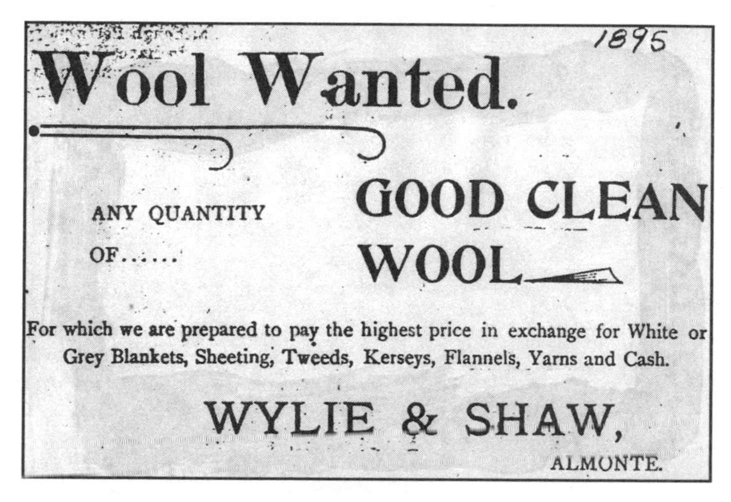

Advertisements for two of Almonte's key woollen factories. The No. 1 Mill was also known as the Rosamond Mill.

Lewis W. Hine's famous photo shows a young worker in a cotton factory in an Augusta, Georgia, mill.

A doffer girl pushes a bin stacked with dozens of bobbins full of cotton yarn. As soon as bobbins became full, workers would replace them with empty bobbins.

Two very young workers in a Georgia textile mill in 1909.

Three doffer girls in a New England mill. Girls often tied their hair back to keep it from getting caught in the huge moving machinery.

Doffer boys at a cotton mill in Macon, Georgia, are covered in bits of cotton.

A twelve-year-old mill worker stands in the spooling room of a Texas cotton mill.

Workers in a cotton mill in Marysville, New Brunswick (now a suburb of Fredericton).

REPORT

OF THE

ROYAL COMMISSION

ON THE

RELATIONS OF LABOR AND CAPITAL

IN

CANADA

The report of the *Royal Commission on the Relations of Labor and Capital,* published in 1889, showed underage workers still being employed in various industries. Its recommendation that children under fourteen not be employed was often disregarded.

This stamp was issued in 1998 to commemorate the anti-child-labour campaign of the early twentieth century. The photo by Lewis Hine is of twelve-year-old Addie, a mill worker in North Pownal, Vermont.

Activist Craig Kielburger (top, centre) founded Free The Children in 1995 when he was just twelve. He had read about young Iqbal Masih (above, right), a Pakistani boy who was sold into slavery at age four, and murdered at age twelve after speaking out about children's rights. Iqbal worked twelve hours a day, six days a week, tying tiny knots to make carpets.

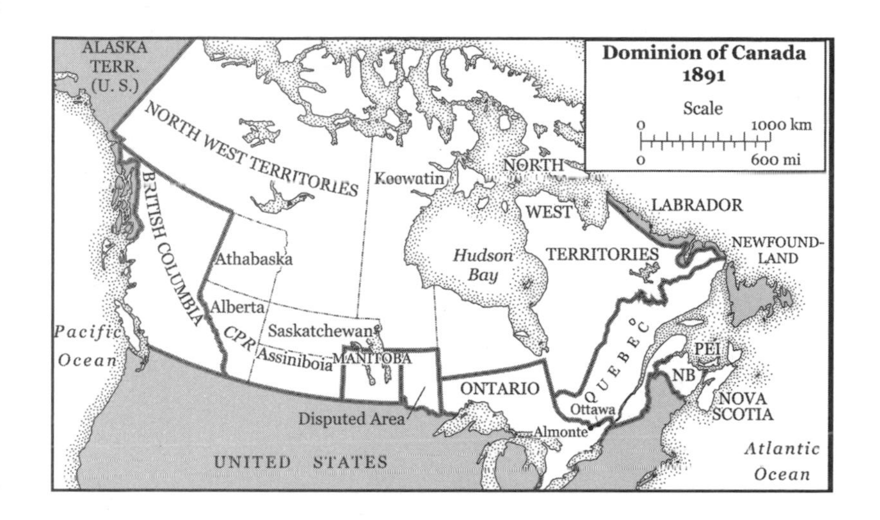

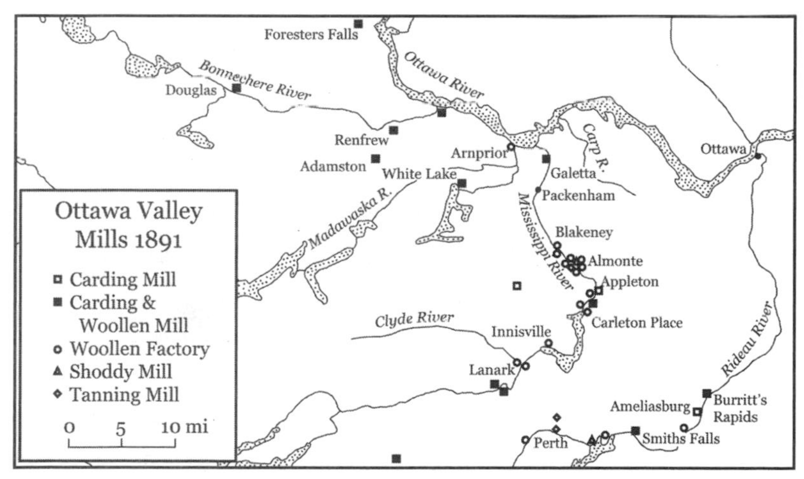

Much of Canada's textile industry was concentrated in the Ottawa River Valley. There were also a number of mills in New Brunswick, Nova Scotia, Quebec and Ontario's Grand River area from Hespeler to Dunnville. Dominion Woollens at Hespeler employed hundreds.

Acknowledgments

Grateful acknowledgment is made for permission to reprint the following:

Cover portrait: (detail) *Avant le bain* by William Bouguereau.
Cover background: detail (colourized), *Victoria Woollen Mills, Almonte, James Rosamond Esq Proprietor,* courtesy of Michael Dunn.

Page 125: "We, who must toil and spin," by Lucy Larcom from *An Idyll of Work,* 1875.
Page 200: *No. 1 Mill, Almonte, Ontario*, Gerald Tennant, courtesy of Michael Dunn.
Page 201: Photo courtesy of the author.
Page 202: Courtesy of Michael Dunn.
Page 203 (upper and lower): Mississippi Valley Textile Museum, courtesy of Michael Dunn.
Page 204: *Little Spinner in Mill, Augusta, GA, 1909,* Lewis W. Hine, George Eastman House, GEH NEG 2505.
Page 205: American Textile History Museum, P227.38294.
Page 206: Georgia mill workers, Lewis Hine.
Page 207: American Textile History Museum, P2212.5.
Page 208: Georgia doffer boys, Lewis Hine.
Page 209: Selina Wall in the Brozos Mill, Texas, Lewis Hine.
Page 210: *Marysville Cotton Mill. Mill workers, including children, posed around machinery to have picture taken, ca 1885 or 1886,* George Taylor, Provincial Archives of New Brunswick, P5-416.
Page 211 (upper): Detail from title page of the *Report of the Royal Commission on the Relations of Labor and Capital.*
Page 211 (lower): *Spinner in New England Mill, 1913,* Lewis W. Hine, stamp issued February 3, 1998.

Page 212 (upper): Craig Kielburger and (lower) Iqbal Masih, courtesy of Free The Children.

Page 213: Map by Paul Heersink/Paperglyphs. Map data © 2000 Government of Canada with permission from Natural Resources Canada. Additional references for the detailed map are from a publication of the North Lanark Historical Society © 1978.

The publisher would like to thank Dr. Joy Parr for providing her expertise on the manuscript. She is the author of *Labouring Children: British Immigrant Apprentices to Canada, 1869–1924,* as well as *The Gender of Breadwinners*, a book about the textile families of Paris, Ontario. She is the editor of two collections on children's history, *Childhood and Family in Canadian History* and *Histories of Canadian Children and Youth*. Thanks also to Michael Dunn for the generous use of his collection of Almonte photographs and for supplying map references, and to Barbara Hehner for her valuable assistance in fact-checking the manuscript.

For Delaney, whose olden days are yet to come

Thanks to the staff of the American Textile History Museum; the Mississippi Valley Textile Museum; Mississippi Mills Public Library, Almonte Branch; Keith Bunnell of the University of British Columbia Library; Vera Rosenbluth and the other generous members of the Association of Personal Historians; and Ruth McBride for her hospitality in Almonte.

About the Author

Sarah Ellis has a rare talent for creating characters that readers identify with so closely, it's as if they're making a new friend. Ivy Weatherall in *A Prairie as Wide as the Sea,* Polly Toakley in *Pick-Up Sticks,* Megan in *Out of the Blue* and Jessica Robertson in *The Baby Project* will be familiar to many young readers.

Once Sarah had decided on a topic for her second Dear Canada book, she travelled to Almonte, Ontario, to do research at the Mississippi Valley Textile Museum, because Almonte was one of the key mill towns in Canada in the late 1800s. One item she saw there helped her create the character of Flora and the conflicts that a young mill worker like Flora might have in her life. In the museum Sarah saw "a beautiful set of doll's clothes, made by a young girl in the late nineteenth century. Adjacent to this display are examples of the various huge, heavy machines used in the mill in the same period. This juxtaposition of the delicate and the mighty led me to thinking about work and industrialization. I thought about the girl who had made the doll's clothes, likely a middle-class child with time to play. I thought about the girl who laboured in the mill, a working-class child whose days were regulated by the rhythm of the machine and the demands of industry. A story was cooking."

Another "find" in Almonte was pure coincidence. An avid gardener, Sarah took a break from researching Flora's story to visit a garden full of irises. There she met a man who had worked for many years in the Ministry of Heritage and who knew all the local history people to contact. "I came home with odd little notes saying *fireflies, leeches, fishing, flour-sack underwear.*" All these eventually made their way into Flora's diary.

Sarah Ellis's first Dear Canada book, *A Prairie as Wide as the Sea,* was a CLA Honour Book. Sarah has a gift for writing in diary format. She tells a story about standing in front of a group of grade ones, talking to them about a book written in diary form, and asking, "Now, does anybody know what a diary is?" "Yes," said a shy little girl, "it's when you don't feel well in your stomach and you have to go to the bathroom in a big hurry."

Sarah has won the Governor General's Award (for *Pick-Up Sticks*) and twice been a finalist (for *Out of the Blue* and *The Several Lives of Orphan Jack*). She has also won the Mr. Christie's Book Award, the IODE Violet Downey Award, the Vicky Metcalf Award for Body of Work, the Sheila Egoff Award and the TD Canadian Children's Literature Award. Her books have been selected as OLA Best Bets, ALA Notables and SLJ Best Books. Sarah is the author of over a dozen children's books, including *The Baby Project, Back of Beyond, Big Ben, The Young Writer's Companion, The Queen's Feet* and *Odd Man Out.*

In addition to her own writing, Sarah lectures on children's literature, teaches writing, and reviews children's books for various publications.

While the events described and some of the characters in this book may be based on actual historical events and real people, Flora Rutherford is a fictional character created by the author, and her diary is a work of fiction.

Library and Archives Canada Cataloguing in Publication

Ellis, Sarah
Days of toil and tears : the child labour diary of Flora Rutherford / Sarah Ellis.

(Dear Canada)
ISBN 978-0-439-95594-2

1. Child labor--Ontario--Almonte--Juvenile fiction.
2. Almonte (Ont.)--Juvenile fiction. I. Title. II. Series.

PS8559.L57D39 2008 jC813'.54 C2007-904461-1

ISBN 0-439-95594-7

6 5 4 3 2 1 Printed in Canada 08 09 10 11 12

The display type was set in Plantagenet Cherokee.
The text was set in Bembo.

First printing January 2008

Alone in an Untamed Land, The Filles du Roi Diary of Hélène St. Onge by Maxine Trottier

Banished from Our Home, The Acadian Diary of Angélique Richard by Sharon Stewart

Brothers Far from Home, The World War I Diary of Eliza Bates by Jean Little

The Death of My Country, The Plains of Abraham Diary of Geneviève Aubuchon by Maxine Trottier

Footsteps in the Snow, The Red River Diary of Isobel Scott by Carol Matas

If I Die Before I Wake, The Flu Epidemic Diary of Fiona Macgregor by Jean Little

No Safe Harbour, The Halifax Explosion Diary of Charlotte Blackburn by Julie Lawson

Not a Nickel to Spare, The Great Depression Diary of Sally Cohen by Perry Nodelman

An Ocean Apart, The Gold Mountain Diary of Chin Mei-ling by Gillian Chan

Orphan at My Door, The Home Child Diary of Victoria Cope by Jean Little

A Prairie as Wide as the Sea, The Immigrant Diary of Ivy Weatherall by Sarah Ellis

Prisoners in the Promised Land, The Ukrainian Internment Diary of Anya Soloniuk by Marsha Skrypuch

A Rebel's Daughter, The 1837 Rebellion Diary of Arabella Stevenson by Janet Lunn

A Ribbon of Shining Steel, The Railway Diary of Kate Cameron by Julie Lawson

A Season for Miracles, Twelve Tales of Christmas

A Trail of Broken Dreams, The Gold Rush Diary of Harriet Palmer by Barbara Haworth-Attard

Turned Away, The World War II Diary of Devorah Bernstein by Carol Matas

Whispers of War, The War of 1812 Diary of Susanna Merritt by Kit Pearson

Winter of Peril, The Newfoundland Diary of Sophie Loveridge by Jan Andrews

With Nothing But Our Courage, The Loyalist Diary of Mary MacDonald by Karleen Bradford